He scooped her up in his arms.

"I've always wanted to do this," he said, breathing hard.

Bay wrapped her arms around his neck, kissing the droplets of seawater there. "Gee, in the movies it never looked like it was any effort."

Paul groaned, dropping her gently onto the grass. "So much for my impression of Burt Lancaster," he said. "You're a lot more solid than you look."

She smiled sweetly. "Diplomatic choice of words. Deborah Kerr wasn't carried, that I recall."

Bay laughed softly, aroused, exhilarated by every aspect of him. His wit, his unconscious charm were as sexy as his body, which now ignited her by moving to within millimeters of her overheated skin.

"Take me," she cried with all the melodrama she could muster, "from here to eternity."

He did.

D0591839

Dear Reader:

SILHOUETTE DESIRE is an exciting new line of contemporary romances from Silhouette Books. During the past year, many Silhouette readers have written in telling us what other types of stories they'd like to read from Silhouette, and we've kept these comments and suggestions in mind in developing SILHOUETTE DESIRE.

DESIREs feature all of the elements you like to see in a romance, plus a more sensual, provocative story. So if you want to experience all the excitement, passion and joy of falling in love, then SILHOUETTE DESIRE is for you.

For more details write to:

Jane Nicholls
Silhouette Books
PO Box 236
Thornton Road
Croydon
Surrey
CR9 3RU

LESLIE DAVIS GUCCIONE
Before the Wind

Silhouette Desire

Originally Published by Silhouette Books
division of
Harlequin Enterprises Ltd.

First published in Great Britain in 1986 by Silhouette Books, 15–16 Brook's Mews, London W1A 1DR

© Leslie Davis Guccione 1986

Silhouette, Silhouette Desire and Colophon are Trade Marks of Harlequin Enterprises B.V.

ISBN 0 373 50443 8

22–1086

Printed and bound in Great Britain by Cox & Wyman Ltd, Reading

LESLIE DAVIS GUCCIONE

lives with her husband and three children in a state of semichaos in an historic district south of Boston where sea captains used to live. When she's not at her typewriter, she's actively researching everything from sailboats to cranberry bogs. What free time she has is spent sailing, and restoring her circa 1827 Cape Cod cottage. Her ideas for her books are based on the world around her. As she states, "Romance is right under your nose." She has also written under the name Leslie Davis.

For my parents
who had the good sense to introduce me to boats
about the time they introduced me to solid food
and
Dorothy Allen Arnold & Andrea Allen Turin
who made spinning this yarn possible

One

Whitney Bay Chandler tapped her foot and tried to
focus on something besides the guests who glanced at
her as they climbed the gracious granite steps leading to
Sea Mist, where the social event of the Newport, Rhode
Island, season was already in full swing. What she chose
was a startlingly attractive blond man standing on the
steps of the mansion.

His hands were in the pockets of his formal trousers,
whose satin stripe picked up the reflection of the flood-
lights as he moved. Halfway down he stopped, resting
his thigh against the balustrade, and looked at the
stream of limousines pulling up to the fountain. This
was no ordinary face, and he reminded Bay of a model
in a cigarette ad except that he wasn't smoking. He
looked bored and exceedingly handsome. When he
turned in her direction, she was jolted out of her reverie, afraid that he had caught her staring. Half-a-dozen

couples passed between them, however, and he gave no indication that he knew he was being observed. After a moment, his hands still in his pockets, he followed the guests into the fabled mansion.

"I'm back, Kiddo." The voice of her brother jolted her and she turned to him.

"Jeremy, I can't go in."

"Of course you can. I didn't go all the way back to the car for the invitation just to have you balk on me now. What would the folks say?"

"They're all in Bermuda, so who's to know?"

In reply Jeremy patted her bare arm and tucked it properly into the crook of his elbow as they began to climb the staircase. With her free hand Bay discreetly pressed the satin bow covering the strapless bodice of her gown, trying to quell her nervousness. Sea Mist, in all its ostentatious splendor, was about to engulf them. Like a heavily made-up dowager past her prime, the cavernous, ornate rooms welcomed the best and brightest of Eastern sailing society on the eve of the Newport–Bermuda Race.

As he had done every other year since college, Jeremy was crewing for a contender. Bay was seeing him off, and the rest of the family was awaiting his arrival in Hamilton, the childhood home of their mother, Fiona Robson Chandler.

That Bay and her ex-husband, Breck Scofield, had once belonged in this society like sloops nestled in a safe harbor did little to calm the butterflies flinging themselves against her stomach. Neither did the fact that her size A bosom was floating around inside the roomy designer gown. At five feet five inches Bay was hopelessly underendowed. She wasn't ashamed that her cleavage was created by half-a-box of tissues in the bottom of the strapless bra—she was quite fond of her slender figure. Bouncing breasts were the last thing she needed when working a yacht in the overwhelmingly male world of chartering in the Virgin Islands. Her problem was simply that the dress, a stunningly slinky satin, had been bought that morning with no time to sew the tuck or two (maybe three) needed to keep her from exposing the point where she stopped and the tissues began. She did not want to worry about it; she had more important things on her mind, such as her not-so-recent divorce, her sudden return after five years in St. Thomas and the problem of explaining it all to the people she would see at this party.

"Damned fishbowl," she muttered, moving her hand from the bodice and fluffing her wild brown curls. "I can't believe I let you talk me into this."

Jeremy presented the engraved invitation he had had to retrieve from his Triumph. More than any of the other Chandlers, Jeremy knew what lay beneath his sister's disposition and that her fiercely independent streak and her aloof air came not from confidence but defeat. He was thirty-eight, and the ten years that separated them gave him enough distance—and experience—to be an excellent judge of Bay's character. His perceptiveness drove her crazy.

The ecru invitation went on the silver tray. "Bay, you used to set Newport on its ear. Nothing's changed in five years except that you're pushing thirty and getting too old for some of your antics."

"Twenty-eight, and plenty has changed. Half the people in that ballroom were at my wedding, watching Breck and me sail off into the sunset. The marriage ran aground, Jemmy. We sank. They probably want their rice and rose petals back, not to mention the wedding presents.''

They moved in the direction of the receiving line. She put on a smile.

''You're being tough on yourself, as usual. This is a party, remember? Have fun. You've been divorced for two years. Nobody wants anything but your happiness.''

''Spare me.''

''We have. Three years with Breck, two without him, and all of it in St. Thomas... It's time you broke out of that Caribbean cocoon and came back to life. You've worked overtime at making us think that chartering yachts was all you wanted from life.''

''And why shouldn't it be?''

''Because you're a Chandler, not a Scofield.''

''You never liked Breck.''

One set of hazel eyes looked at the other. ''I like him fine, as a crack sailor, a hellraiser, navigator...just not as your husband. You and I are peas from the same pod, Kiddo. Life in the fast lane doesn't have the same appeal for us as it does for Breck. Frankly, you're a lot more mature than he'll ever be, if you want my opinion.''

''I don't want your opinion,'' she threw back in a stage whisper as she stepped forward to extend her hand to the hostess, ''especially when it includes a 'you're not living up to your potential' lecture.''

Jeremy grinned as Bay greeted the eighty-year-old grande dame cordially, then moved on to shake hands with the gentleman next in line.

''What you need,'' he stated in subdued tones, ''is what Mother calls a 'fling.' ''

No sooner were the words out of his mouth than she thought of the man on the steps. Bay's cheeks flamed while she ignored her sibling and made small talk with the next couple, who asked about her parents and wished her brother smooth sailing in the upcoming race.

When they were finally out of earshot, she gave him a withering look. "Honestly, you have some nerve. Stay out of my private life."

"You don't have one, love. You've done a great job of convincing Mom and Dad and even Christopher of how full and fabulous your life has been down there. I don't buy it. Never did."

"Jeremy—"

"Have some champagne." He grabbed two glasses from a tray. "Then come and have the first dance with me and pick up some dashing anonymous bachelor in there."

Bay gulped the drink and looked away from the crowded ballroom, back to her tormentor. "How does Nancy put up with you?"

"Ah," he sighed, "devotion. We're not talking about my marriage tonight, nor Chris's. You should know, however, that as soon as we're back from Hamilton, Nancy wants to have the pediatrician to dinner. Both your brothers and both your sisters-in-law..."

"No blind dates!"

"When was the last time you had a real date?"

"I mean it," she threw back, ignoring his remark. "I'm home for the solitude."

"The hell with solitude, little sister. Take my advice. Forget for the moment about love. Forget about forever and for heaven's sake, forget about Breck. Practice tonight. Bat those green eyes, flounce your stuff! Find somebody you'll never see again and live a little."

Her green eyes widened in feigned offense. "My *stuff* does not flounce. You're disgusting, you know that? And while we're on the subject, there's nobody here I wouldn't see again. If I lived a little, as you say, he'd probably turn out to be an old fraternity brother of Breck's or the son of Mother's tennis partner."

She sighed under the strain, trying to deny the concern behind her brother's teasing. "And so help me, Jeremy Chandler, if you invite somebody to dinner—a baby doctor or anyone else without telling me—I'll be back in St. Thomas before you can set the table."

They drained their glasses, and Jeremy put them down on the bench where they had settled. "Righteous indignation makes you gorgeous. Don't waste it on your big brother. I was not suggesting major scandal, just a little Scarlett O'Hara. There must be a Rhett Butler in there somewhere."

Whitney Bay Chandler stuck out her tongue.

She wasn't gorgeous in the conventional sense and was certainly not conventional. Whitney Bay was named for the deserted stretch of Bermudian beach where she had been conceived on her parents' second honeymoon, and she strongly favored her mother's side of the family. Too short to be considered willowy and too tall for perky, at five-five the adjective *striking* suited her physical appearance and described her character well.

She had her mother's eyes and a perfect pair of sea legs beneath her small-breasted athletic torso. Although she considered herself burned out emotionally, the constant demands of running fifty-foot yachts kept her in excellent physical condition. The one exception to that was her feet. Barefoot or with her feet encased in Topsiders, she could work a twenty-hour day.

Pressed into kid sling-back sandals, her toes were screaming after three hours on the ballroom floor at Sea Mist.

It was nearly midnight. After the first waltz Jeremy had handed her over to a second cousin. There had been an usher from her wedding and lots of small talk with acquaintances who had heard through the grapevine that she was no longer a Scofield. Now, as the clock struck twelve, she was gingerly pulling her sandaled feet from under the Florentine patent leather dress shoes of an Italian *comandante*.

Where the devil was Prince Charming when you needed him? So much for living a little.

"Scusi."

She winced. "That's quite all right, Signor de Parma." They were nearly equal in height, but whereas Bay was lithe, the *comandante* was lumbering, and he moved cheerfully across the floor like a stuffed teddy bear. His English was excellent, his credentials impressive. Unfortunately his dancing was atrocious, and he was becoming too familiar, to boot. Closer to her ear than she would have liked, he was murmuring about the superb reputation of Chandler Sails.

The orchestra was halfway through "Some Enchanted Evening," Bay was scanning the room for a handsome stranger and *Comandante* de Parma was stepping on her right foot. She clutched his shoulder for balance as he steered her into a pivot.

There he was. His arms folded across his chest, her blond fantasy stood against the doorframe. There was a half smile on his face as though he'd been enjoying the scenario, but as Bay put on her best SOS expression, he moved through the crowd, his thick hay-colored hair bobbing in the sea of tuxedos.

Her attention was diverted by Neapolitan fingers tentatively counting her vertebrae. Bay's spine tingled, but not from the *comandante*'s touch. Her pulse quickened as she caught sight of the blonde again. He was now twenty feet away, at the edge of the bar.

"Once you have found him, never let him go...." The *comandante* was singing the lyrics, whispering them, actually, into her temple. His attempt at cheek-to-cheek seduction gave her a chance to study the blonde. At first glance he appeared to be a clone of one of the hundreds of dashing, rich sea lovers who were filling the great house.

His handsome head of hair, however, had neither the benign neglect of those who answered only to the winds and tides nor the salon finish of the power brokers in the ballroom. His was a plain corner-barbershop cut.

Where the upper crust wore their formal dress as casually as old L. L. Bean chamois shirts and added madras, citrus-colored linen or brocade for accent, the blonde's attire was conventional. His cummerbund, bow tie, dinner jacket and satin-striped dress pants all were black.

Bay Chandler, whether she would admit it or not, could pigeonhole anybody into the appropriate social class from fifty yards, especially in a room filled with old money, new money, and those aspiring to one of the two. That was what kept her glance returning to the faintly cynical face across the room; he fit no category.

His ensemble was obviously rented, and she had yet to see him speak to a soul. If Bay had competition, she couldn't spot it. Mentally she dressed him in jeans and a polo shirt and then a three-piece suit, trying to decide what would look more natural on his trim frame. It made her face hot.

Her reverie was brought to an abrupt halt as the moist fingers reached the satin-covered buttons at the base of her spine. She stopped in her tracks.

"Signor Comandante!"

"Por favore. On this enchanted evening, you must call me Enzo. There is new color in your cheeks, the beating of your pulse...see how it pounds in your throat? You are feeling it, *sì?"*

Her hand flew to her cheek. *"Signor.* Enzo, I think it's time we found my brother. Jeremy will be delighted to see you again. He's racing an Italian-designed boat on Monday...." She kept up the banter as they snaked their way through the dancers, the ballroom, the foyer and into the mahogany-paneled library, where Jeremy and his fellow crewmen were avoiding the dancing.

As financier of a racing syndicate, the *comandante* was welcomed, and Bay squeezed her brother's hand gratefully.

"So, Kiddo, have you—"

"Don't ask." Her green eyes flashed at his, and she left.

She was walking with a noticeable limp along the parquet floor. The bar was now occupied by half-a-dozen couples. The object of her fantasizing was gone.

Just as well, she thought sourly. It was well past the pumpkin hour, and she was genuinely exhausted. She hobbled toward the open French doors in search of a spot to remove her sandals. She had half a mind to yank out the tissue, as well, and leave it under one of the manicured boxwood hedges.

Bay stepped onto the broad flagstone terrace. Unwisely she was sipping another drink, but with the balance that comes from living aboard a ship she bent over, pulling one then the other sandal from her aching feet. Not a drop of champagne was spilled.

"Find somebody you'll never see again and live a little." Jeremy's advice hovered in her mind. How romantic it would have been. Deep in discussion over battens and grommets with Comandante de Parma, the only daughter of sailmaker John Chandler was suddenly whisked from her partner's arms by a handsome blond stranger. The guests made room as she moved into his waiting embrace, and they waltzed to appreciative applause before retreating to the waiting coach. Love-starved divorcée saved from crushing boredom by... whom?

Whom, indeed. Bay blinked. Some seductress she was. She hadn't even been able to catch his attention. That placid high-boned face seemed always to be glancing just above eye level. Whatever he had been concentrating on, it certainly hadn't been her.

If she didn't know *who* he was, her reverie told her *what* he was. There was always the chance that he was a reporter covering the opening of another Newport season as he tried to blend unobtrusively with the guests. More likely, however, he was an undercover security guard for the Preservation Society to whose care Sea Mist and its enormous neighbors were entrusted.

Bay's introduction to security guards had been during her summer as a debutante. Hired by parents to mingle among the hundreds of college-age hellions, their duties were simple: keep the debutantes and their escorts out of the bushes, the champagne in the hands of those of legal age and the silver on the table.

But tonight the bushes were empty, and the crowd behind her was subdued. Low indirect lighting from the manicured plants cast deep shadows, and what moonlight there was, was splintered on the rippled water. Impulsively Bay stooped again, and leaving the empty glass on the steps, she gathered the gown up against her legs.

Holding her sandals in one hand and the folds of satin in the other, Bay strolled through the grass, letting the cool dampness bring her feet back to life. The stimulation tingled along her calves, her thighs, and lifted her spirits as she made her way across the wide expanse of lawn.

She reached the edge of the steep bluff beyond which stretched the vast Atlantic Ocean, and without a second thought, she tossed her too-tight, too-fashionable sandals into the night.

She imagined them sinking dramatically to the depths of the foaming brine, but on closer inspection she realized the tide was out. Bay leaned over, squinting into the darkness. The sandals had fallen unceremoniously on the rocks below her.

It had been a hasty decision. They had cost a fortune and were the only dressy shoes she owned. Inspired by the quantity of champagne she had consumed and that was now affecting her judgment, Bay hiked her gown up, swung her leg over the pedestrian rail and was about to slide down the embankment to the beach when she was grabbed roughly from behind. At the unexpected manhandling she threw her elbows back, and they landed soundly in a cushion of ribs and diaphragm. She spun around to face her abductor. "Don't touch me!"

"Believe me," came the coughing reply, "I wouldn't dream of it. A stab in the gut is what I deserve for trying to rescue a floundering woman from the edge of a cliff. You looked rather despondent."

"Despondent!" Bay sputtered, opening her eyes wide in the dark to make sure the vision in front of her was whom she thought. Fright melted away to be replaced by such a wildly racing heart that she thought her pitiful cleavage must be palpitating over the top of the white satin.

His strong fingers left her bare arm to run through his clipped tangle of yellow hair and then press down the pleats of his formal dress shirt. "Are you all right? You looked like you were slipping off the railing."

"Fine," she replied, "and hardly despondent. I threw my shoes down there. I had no idea anyone was lurking in the shadows."

Her anonymous blond fantasy looked out at the ocean and then back into her face, despite her attempt to look away. "I wasn't lurking. I was on the terrace when you came through. You were barely ten feet from me when you pulled off your shoes, never spilling a drop of champagne from the glass." He shook his head. "Hell of a first impression, Cinderella."

Bay stood transfixed, flushed, her entire digestive system reduced to a knot of nerves. Her gorgeous hunk of anonymity had sprung to life, depositing himself at her feet. Now what!

Her eyes fell to his hand just as he was about to reach out to touch the fabric molded to her by the sea breeze. Instead he pulled off his dinner jacket and draped it over her shoulders.

"My, you are Prince Charming," she managed.

"I can't stand to see a woman shivering in the cold."

Bay did not have the nerve to tell him her condition had nothing to do with the temperature of the air. Instead she looked up into his moonlit face. His strong jaw was as ill-suited to a tuxedo as the rest of him. An introspective air lingered on his features, though his smile was deep and sincere. She wondered what color his eyes were.

"I suppose you're going to give me a lecture about crossing over the railing."

He shrugged. "It's pitch-black out here. You could have broken your neck on the way down. The railing's there for a purpose. Perhaps we should get back."

She nodded. So much for blond fantasies. Security guard eases despondent party-goer from edge of cliff. All in a night's work. Her pulse was beginning to slow as they walked leisurely across the manicured grass. Bay was feeling more like an awkward teenager and less like an independent yacht captain by the minute. The magnetic attraction to this handsome misfit was so unwarranted that she felt as though she were in someone else's body.

His voice was soft. "You danced out here like a sprite. You'll have to forgive me for wanting a closer look."

"I suppose I should ask you to forgive me for crossing the railing."

"You did look as though you were losing your balance."

"My balance is fine. My brother didn't send you out here, did he?" She blurted out the words the moment it occurred to her that dear Jeremy might very probably have scouted around for suitable "fling material" for his kid sister.

"Do I know your brother?"

"I hope not," Bay finished, wishing she'd forgone the last glass of champagne.

He didn't seem to notice her tipsiness. "I haven't done much socializing. Who's your brother?"

Oh, no you don't, Bay thought gloomily. Here come the connections, the Chandler name, family business, Newport ties, inevitable link to Breck, failed marriage, noncareer, almost thirty with nothing to show but battle scars. . . .

She stared up into his dark eyes, letting her head swim with a stream of images. Then again, maybe to a security guard the names Scofield or Chandler wouldn't mean a thing.

She found herself once again imagining him in clothes other than formal dress. Her head cocked slightly while she admired the head of hair that had first caught her eye. His jacket was engulfing her, and in the white pleated shirt his shoulders seemed broad, as did his chest, rising and falling with the rhythms of his even breathing.

He crossed his arms over his chest, as she had seen him do in the ballroom.

"Do I pass inspection?" he asked without a trace of discomfort.

Looking away, Bay stammered, "Forgive me. I was trying to decide whether we'd met."

His chin rose as he looked up at the imposing estate. "I'd remember, Cinderella. Not very likely. Not very likely at all. These things—" he paused, sweeping his arm to encompass the house and its guests "—are my idea of torture."

The gesture included Bay, and she stiffened defensively. "I'm not crazy about them either, but you could have done more to socialize inside."

"Well, well—" his blond head turned in her direction "—have you been keeping an eye on me?"

She bit her lip again. "Of course not. At one point in the evening, my dancing partner nearly trampled me, but you seemed oblivious."

"You're probably right. I was concentrating more on the architecture than the guests. Some house," he finished flatly.

"Completely overdone," Bay said, continuing the impersonal subject. "Have you been here before?"

He shook his head. "Hard to believe, but I never had the interest. My grandparents spent their entire lives here, but I had never set foot in it."

Bay kept walking to hide her confusion. If his family had been part of Sea Mist's lively past, then the link to the Robsons and Chandlers was even closer than she'd thought. So much for anonymous strangers. She'd been right when she told Jeremy that they always turned out to have a connection.

Bay's voice changed completely, taking on a casual tone as she tried to pretend he was of no more interest than the *comandante*. "No doubt our grandparents knew each other, then. Mine were here as well. The Robsons probably played croquet right here with your family." Ugh. She was indulging in the sort of idle chitchat she despised, but the attempt to dismiss her attraction to him failed miserably.

He laughed lightly, touching her shoulder. "Not likely, Cinderella. My grandfather was the chauffeur, my grandmother, the cook. I doubt they had time for lawn activities."

Even her Caribbean tan could not hide the crimson creeping across her cheeks. "I didn't mean to embarrass you," she offered.

With deliberate interest he looked from her eyes to her mouth. "From the looks of things, you're doing the blushing." They had reached the terrace, and he stooped for her empty glass.

"What a breath of fresh air you are, Miss Robson. May I get you another drink?"

"Yes, but I'm not," Bay answered, referring to the fact that her last name was Chandler, not Robson.

"Oh, but you are," he said, referring to his comment about the fresh air.

She stood alone on the flagstone as he disappeared through the French doors. "Damn you, Jeremy," she said out loud for lack of anyone else to blame. Inside the doors the orchestra was playing, and Bay had to smile at herself. She had guessed correctly. She was flirting with the hired help—Granny Robson would have died.

He returned with two tumblers and handed one to Bay. "Ginger ale. I'm still on call, and I thought you might like one, as well."

The implication that she'd had enough champagne was unmistakable. All in a night's work, she thought sourly.

He put his glass on the terrace railing. "Would you accept a dance as an apology for my scaring you to death out there?"

Bay smiled, as the adrenaline began to flow again. "Can you risk it?"

"Are you that bad?" he asked.

Bay laughed. "I meant since you're working."

He looked at his watch. "I'm fine. I have a few minutes—" His arms opened expectantly.

Without another word she moved into them. That he held her the proper distance, one hand high between her shoulder blades, was no surprise. The shock was the smoothness with which he moved. Effortlessly, never so

much as scraping her bare feet, he led her over the cool
flagstones. They swayed in perfect rhythm as she followed the delicious hints of his body, forward then
back.

The knot inside her began to loosen, melting from the
perfect pressure of his arms. Like the sun in the islands
it permeated her with radiating warmth.

A part of Bay hoped that he would remain the proper
gentleman, thank her and disappear as easily as he had
arrived. Something deeper, however, wanted to cling,
longing to be brought back to life.

Beneath her left hand his right shoulder moved as his
arms tightened and loosened. His fingertips on her
back, pressing then releasing her, sent deep waves of
emotion into her limbs. As the music slowed, they
reached a darkened corner next to the house, and the
proper distance they had maintained fell away.

Thigh-to-thigh, they moved to the strains of the orchestra, and his left hand now pressed her right next to
his heart. The thick blond hair that had first drawn her
attention now drifted through her open fingers, filling
Bay with a delicious sense of risk.

A barely discernable pressure on her back brought
her into him as his hand slid to the rise of her buttocks.
His fingers brushed the satin and waited, a movement
identical to the *comandante*'s but this time, finding
Jeremy was the furthest thought from Bay's mind.

By the time he leaned toward her, Bay's eyes were
closed, her chin tilted in anticipation. His lips brushed
her eyes, then he pressed a kiss lightly on her forehead.
She opened her eyes to find him staring at her.

Under his scrutiny, the color rose to her face again,
and he moaned softly. His firm, lean fingers uncurled

on either side of her face, pushing her brown curls back from her temples.

As if he were memorizing her features, his eyes moved over the planes of her face and touched on Bay's chin, cheeks, the bridge of her nose. On his wrist the watch buzzed, dramatically breaking the spell.

"Stay with me," he implored. "I have to make a phone call. I'll be back."

They stared into each other's eyes for an instant, and then he was crushing her to his chest. Like a departing soldier, he found her mouth, already parted in anticipation, and kissed her hard. Their tongues, gliding, teasing, hinting at more, explored with abandon.

When they parted, it was with breathless laughter. "Stay with me," he commanded, kissing her once more.

Bay smiled and picked his dinner jacket off the terrace where it had slid off her shoulders. She caught sight of the Newport Formals rental label as she handed it to him.

Bay stood stock-still, trying to make sense of it, catching her breath. No one had touched her like this— let alone a perfect stranger. Five minutes stretched to ten. Stay with him? Hadn't she taken this innocent flirtation as far as she dared? She didn't even know his name!

A hugely romantic interlude on the terrace of a mansion was one thing. A night in some unknown apartment was quite another. And then there was always the morning. . . .

Her passion cooled to excitement. She'd have to tell Jeremy it had been wonderful practice in the lost art of seduction. Bay smiled then frowned, remembering his threat of blind dates once she was home.

Excitement cooled to reality. She was freezing, barefooted and tipsy. Twenty minutes was long enough. Let it pass as a lovely silly interlude, she thought, now that she had proved to herself that she was still able to attract a devastatingly attractive man.

She waited twenty-five minutes, thought that fair enough then went through the doors in search of her brother.

She found him in the library, and he was as anxious to leave as she. "Do I dare ask where you've been?" he asked, grinning at her bare feet and disheveled hair.

There was not a hint of a blush this time. "Out being seduced by the hired help."

Two

―

Jeremy handled rounds of boisterous goodbyes as Bay, still shoeless, eased her way down to the steps. At last they got into into Jeremy's Triumph and headed for their cousin's house, where they were houseguests for the weekend. Newport was not home. Alden's Cove, Massachusetts, a two-hour drive northeast, was the center of Chandler Sailmakers and home to Bay's family.

"You must have seen him," she said sleepily over the roar of the engine, "tall, fair, rugged face—"

"Tuxedo, good dancer," her brother finished. "Sorry, Kiddo, you've just described most of the men there tonight. Without Nancy, I was holed up in the library all night."

"That should make her happy." Bay was yawning as they sped toward the Robsons'.

Jeremy put his hand on her arm. "I hope you'll find what Nancy and I have."

Bay smiled at the rare sincerity. "I doubt if I'll find Prince Charming by picking up security guards, Jem. Did I tell you his grandparents were part of Sea Mist's staff?"

"How democratic."

She looked out the window. "He certainly was a fabulous—"

"No details, please."

She turned her head. "I was going to say *dancer*. And if there's a word about this to the family..."

Jeremy's hand went up in assurance.

"Good. I just wanted to prove to you that I'm capable of fending for myself."

"Never doubted it for a minute" were her brother's last words.

The remainder of the weekend was a blur of social activity and emotional upheaval. By the time she saw her brother off in the race, she had lunched, wined, sipped tea and caught up with five years of news from the summer colony of which her blonde did not seem to be a part. Then again, not having the faintest idea what his name was, if someone had mentioned him, she never would have known.

The episode at Sea Mist refused to fade. It lingered, painfully making Bay's heart jump at the sight of a tousled blond head. She searched crowds, watched tourists but never saw him.

Monday morning, with Jeremy out to sea and the rest of the Chandlers awaiting him in Hamilton, Bay faced the fact that it was time to head for Alden's Cove. She had flown from St. Thomas straight to Newport, with her worldly goods stuffed into the rear of her brother's sports car, after he had met her at the airport.

Five years' accumulation amounted to little more than bathing suits, shorts, sundresses and a motley collection of T-shirts emblazoned with off-color slogans. Do It in the Virgins was a gag gift from a pair of grateful honeymooners, and thereafter, departing sailors had added to her collection.

Bay's life had revolved around the tight circle of love couples brought to her boats. Love that included their captain in only the most superficial way. Though she had yet to admit it, Jeremy was right. St. Thomas no longer held anything for her. It was time to call Alden's Cove home again.

She intended to live in her apartment over the boathouse-garage of the Chandler compound. Wedding presents had furnished it, and Fiona had it decorated for Breck and Bay's first Christmas visit.

Now under a cloudless June sky, the red convertible skimmed north along the back roads skirting Cape Cod and Massachusetts bays. The only exception to the inventory in the back seat was the *Respite*, the fifty-one-foot Morgan OutIslander, a wedding present from both families, and the one thing Bay and Breck still owned jointly.

With the roar of the Triumph in her ears, Bay did not ease up on the accelerator until she pulled off the main road onto the lane toward the rocky coastline. Welcome to Alden's Cove, Settled 1634, the sign read. "You win," Bay yelled over the whining gears as she downshifted into second. "I'm back, you codfish-every-Sunday town."

The Chandler Sail Lofts, a series of prominent brick structures perched on the rocks, hemmed in the first of the inlets making up the Cove. Hundreds of boats at anchor filled the bay both here and farther along the shore. There was a restaurant or two, fashionable boutiques and finally the green stretch of the common. The grassy park was lined by stately white captains' houses, each looking out on the Atlantic beyond the bay. None of Newport's grandeur here. Such an ostentatious display would be unthinkable.

The Chandler Compound lay half a mile beyond, off its own lane running to the water. Though her family had been making sails since the China Trade, the original house was now part of the office area. Her great-grandfather gave it up to settle where they still were, on the edge of the village.

Bay did not stop again until she eased the car down the maple-lined drive. The Big House, as it had always been called, came first, the one in which three generations of Chandlers had raised their families. Jeremy and Christopher had each built one of their own, bordering the property to the south, and beyond them all, tucked among a tangle of beach plum, sat the four-bay garage and boathouse with an apartment above. Each home had been built to take advantage of the ocean view. Rolling lawns, rutted drive and landscaping separated one from the other, all eerily quiet as she bounced along the gravel.

The morning was given over to stocking her kitchen and unpacking, but by ten-thirty she was walking the private stretch of beach, kicking shells, wondering what exactly she planned to do now that she was home. After five years of sharing the head, elbow and galley space, the solitude she craved stretched into self-analysis and contemplation. She was not used to having so much time to think.

With the exception of her family, what social ties she had had in the Cove had been severed or gradually diminished with what had been planned as her permanent move to St. Thomas. At lunchtime she made a sandwich and sat on the balcony that ran across the front of her rooms and served as a cap for the structure below. The water out in front of her sparkled with sunlight and sailboats, reminding her to sign up for the Midsummer Series of races due to begin the next Sunday.

By dark she had watched the lawn-care service on its weekly rounds, rearranged the wicker and deck chairs half-a-dozen times, made a quiche and made a mental promise to venture forth in the morning, if for no other reason than to sign up for the races. Her first night at home, alone in her brass bed, was as restless as her day had been. She spent half the night listening to the slap of halyards against metal masts as boats rode their anchors beyond her windows, and half drifting in and out of faintly erotic dreams about blondes looking for lost shoes and champagne bottles. At six-fifteen the next morning, she threw off the sheet.

The amount of time she was giving to thoughts of her anonymous fantasy was beginning to bother her. He's even invading my sleep, was the last thing she said to herself as she stumbled across the living room to the kitchen, zipping up her green shorts as she went.

"Today, Chandler, you get your rear end moving," she said out loud, snapping the refrigerator door closed with her hip for emphasis. She placed a grapefruit on the cutting board and grabbed the only knife in evidence, a serrated blade for bread. Vowing to get over to the yacht club before noon for the sign-up, Bay glanced at the clock as she sliced through the grapefruit. It was barely six forty-five. Hours to go.

Until her palm began to sting from the citric acid, Bay was unaware that anything was wrong. Bringing her gaze back to the grapefruit, however, brought her eyes wide open in surprise and delayed pain. Blood and juice merged into rivulets, running across the counter, the razor-sharp tip of the knife having sliced her palm from thumb to heel.

Instinctively Bay pressed it with her other hand against her ribs, biting her lip against the throbbing. That didn't help and neither did kicking the cabinets with her bare foot. "Damn!" she cried again and again. "Stupid, stupid, stupid."

She held her hand under cold tap water, trying to flush the wound long enough to make a diagnosis. It was obvious that she needed stitches. With her hand clutched against the stained shirt, she lowered her forehead to the edge of the sink. Call a doctor, she told herself. She looked back at the clock: six-fifty. Too early. Call Dr. Cohen anyway, get the answering service . . . wake him up.

Bay wrapped her hand as tightly as she could in a clean linen dish towel and headed for the phone. She hadn't seen the family physician in three years, though his number, in her mother's handwriting, was still taped to the base of the wall phone. She dialed the number, still pressing her teeth into her bottom lip. Bay's eyes were beginning to smart as she rehearsed what she would say to the answering service.

"Dr. Bendette," a male voice said clearly after the second ring.

"Excuse me," she faltered, "is this the answering service for Dr. Cohen?"

The voice continued. "This is Dr. Bendette the pediatrician, Dr. Cohen's partner. May I help you?"

A dime-size crimson stain began to seep through the last layer of toweling as Bay closed her eyes, trying to clear her head. "This is Bay Chandler. I'm an old patient of Dr. Cohen's, and I've cut my hand." Once she began to talk, the words tumbled out in her relief at having reached a doctor.

"I know I need stitches, but I'm alone, and I don't think I can drive all the way to Plymouth General. I was calling to see if—"

"Have you elevated it?" His voice was still professional, but concern etched the question reassuringly.

"Yes," she answered, "but I can't seem to stop the bleeding." After a quick description of the wound, she waited for his suggestion.

"I'm prepared to suture here, if you can make it to the office."

"Dr. Bendette, I'll be there in five minutes. And thanks," she finished, "thanks so much."

Bay tried to think. The car to which she had keys was Jeremy's Triumph. Without even rushing back for sandals, she held the injured hand protectively against her already bloody T-shirt and left the boathouse.

Her beach-toughened feet ran across the gravel and she eased herself into the seat. The rest was torture. Bay was left-handed and the slice was in her right hand, the one with which she had to shift gears.

The engine turned over with the first try, purring then roaring as she attempted to drive along the meandering entrance to the Chandler Compound. With every gravelly bump and twist, pain shot from the injury along the tendons in her wrist. She finally got the car into second gear only to reach the main road and have to start all over.

First, second, then third, and she was heading out to Pilgrim's Point and the medical office used by her entire family. At the halfway mark Bay remembered Jeremy's threat, a blind date with the pediatrician. She was in too much pain to smile, but thought that what she must look like, windblown, bloody and—she glanced at her chest—emblazoned with Divers Do It Deeper, would give even the most love-starved bachelor second thoughts.

She slowed the sports car in front of the clapboard house that housed offices, pushing her palm one last time against the ball of the stick shift. This time the pain was excruciating, and she let the tears stream down her cheeks.

With the exception of a small Ford Escort, the trim parking lot was empty. Bay pulled the Triumph in at a ragged angle, sinking her head onto the steering wheel before getting up.

Whitney Bay Chandler was not the fainting type. In fact, when her ears began to ring with a shrill, piercing whine, she was confused. Raising her head from the steering wheel heightened the pain and wooziness so that she had to blink repeatedly to clear her vision as she got out of the car.

She stumbled to the screen door of the office and leaned on it to keep from falling. By the time she had made it over the threshold, her knees were threatening to buckle.

In less than a minute it was no longer possible to clear her mind. Her pulse was pounding in her temples and in her palm, every pumping sensation sending slivers of pain through her body. While blood seemed to be rushing from the wound, there was little left in her head.

"Dr. Bendette?" came out as a hoarse croak. The waiting room began to spin. She closed her eyes as ringing, then blackness washed over her.

"Good God!" was the last thing she heard as she pitched forward against a muscled chest and into a pair of arms.

"How embarrassing," she managed to whisper.

Bay drifted back to reality as a hand slid under her shirt, pressing something cold against her left breast. She blinked.

Mickey Mouse and Donald Duck were spinning recklessly above her nose with Pluto off to the left. She jammed her eyes shut. "Never Never Land," she mumbled.

The painfully familiar voice of Dr. Bendette said humorlessly, "Welcome back, Cinderella."

Flat on her back on a leather examining table barely wider than her body, Bay lifted her head enough to press her chin into her neck. She looked at the mound of a hand under her T-shirt, holding a stethoscope against her heart, then followed the arm up to the face. The face! It couldn't be. Her eyes snapped shut again.

The moment the stethoscope was removed, Bay bolted into a sitting position and landed once more against the restraining arm of the doctor. "Whoa!" It was a command, and she let herself be eased back onto the table.

With total professionalism her tousle-haired Prince Charming straightened her shirt around her waist and took the instrument from his neck. "A healthy specimen like you should not be fainting over a laceration. Are you pregnant?"

"Of course not," she sputtered, feeling very much like a fly flailing helplessly in a web.

"When's the last time you had a real meal?"

"I don't eat much."

"No, the Chandlers are all in Bermuda. I suppose you're out there at the compound by yourself."

So much for anonymous strangers. "Yes."

"I had no idea you were driving yourself all the way over here. It wasn't a smart thing to do."

"I didn't have much choice, Dr. Bendette." Her voice was rapidly becoming as aloof as his.

The rugged jaw above her clenched as he turned his head and concentrated on the injury. She lay still as he unwrapped the soiled towel and placed her arm gently on a a flat stainless steel tray that he had pulled out from the examining table.

After busying himself with antiseptic and bandages, he settled on the stool beside her. Bay turned, noting the smears of her blood on his otherwise fresh shirt before looking up at his face. Their eyes met. His steely disciplined gaze was pure blue, the color of sea glass.

Color flooded back into her ashen complexion, and she caught the flicker of knowing in his eyes that showed he was aware of the effect he was having. He set to work cleaning the wound.

"I don't understand," she said, biting her lip against the stinging.

"What? That the grandson of servants can study medicine? Life is full of surprises, Miss Chandler. Or is it Miss Robson?"

The flatness of his voice was as painful as the work, and as her eyes filled with tears, she lowered her curly brown lashes and turned her head. The handsome blond fantasy she'd thrown herself at because she'd never see him again was now injecting her hand with novocaine.

"Relax." It was still a command, but his voice had softened. "I know you're uncomfortable, but this will help. Can you feel this?" His touch, even a finger's worth, sent sparks into her. She nodded, and he handed her a tissue without comment.

When her palm was finally free of sensation, his fingers opened hers, splaying them on the sterile cloths. The brief kiss they had shared at Sea Mist ignited memories and . . . her body. She moaned quietly.

"You shouldn't feel much," he said, concentrating on the sutures.

"I wish I didn't."

She lay still, watching Mickey and Donald.

"This is quite a slice. You're more despondent than I realized. Self-inflicted?"

Bay turned her head back, surprised at the touch of humor. "I wasn't aiming for my wrist, Dr. Bendette. I was slicing a grapefruit."

"Why don't you call me Paul?" he replied sarcastically. "We seem to have been on a first-name basis a few nights ago."

"It was a no-name basis," she murmured. "I didn't mean for you to think I was a Robson. Well, I am, but it's my mother's maiden name. Her family was at Sea Mist. I would have told you had you asked."

"Really?" His eyes never left his work. "I recall asking you to wait, a request you ignored."

"You told me you were a security guard. I thought you were working—"

"A security guard—is that what you thought!" Between sutures he paused long enough to give her a withering look. "I said I was *on call*. I went inside to call the hospital. I had a four-year-old in intensive care. Of course it fits, doesn't it? Chauffeur, cook, security guard. Were you doing a little slumming?"

Bay turned her head and with a crumpled tissue wiped the tears that refused to stop, wishing she could yank back her hand and march out of the office—and out of his life.

They fell into an awkward silence as he concentrated on stitching her wound. This was the pediatrician Nancy and Jeremy wanted to fix her up with, Bay realized, looking at the pile of disposable diapers on top of the medicine cabinet. She looked at the infant scale, the eye chart with little sailboats, stars and ducks instead of letters and finally the diplomas and certificates full of neat calligraphy. It was twenty minutes before she spoke again.

"Jean-Paul Bendette, M.D.," she read in her prep-school French.

"Jean-Paul Bendette, M.D.," he corrected in what she knew to be Quebecois. "French Canadian on my father's side, Irish on my mother's. Hearty working-class stock."

"So you said."

Paul shifted his weight, gingerly lifting her hand to examine his work. She followed his glance, looking at his long, neat fingers cradling hers and then at the thin line of tiny black knots. "How many sutures?" she asked, fighting the desire to roll off the table and into his arms.

"Seventeen," he replied, putting an arm around her back and helping her to a sitting position. His deep blue eyes softened as he glanced at her Divers Do It Deeper shirt, bloodstains and all. She could only guess at the contrast she must be presenting from the white-satined sophisticate—bosom and all—to this waif clad in a shirt with an off-color slogan.

The smile she hadn't seen since Sea Mist crossed his face before he turned to move the instruments.

"I sleep in these," she offered weakly. "I have a whole collection given to me by sailors." Small breasts or not, her nipples were erect and sensitive, and clearly defined for his eyes as he looked back at her.

"St. Thomas, isn't it?" The second tidbit dropped as he worked the gauze and adhesive tape around the injury. As numb as the area was, the brushing of his hands, the stroking along the tendons, raised every hair to gooseflesh. She shivered, hunching her shoulders slightly against the obvious desire welling in her. She looked at the eye chart, biting her lip against the tingling.

"Sorry I don't have a dinner jacket this time. You look as though you could use some warming up."

Bastard, she intoned silently. She felt half-naked, defenseless and foolish, but she tossed her proud auburn head as she slid off the table and into the chair next to his desk. Paul sat down.

"Do you always start work so early?" Bay met his eyes again, still amazed that this ruggedly handsome man ministered to children. It would never have occurred to her. Even now he was as illusive as he'd been across the ballroom at Sea Mist—a mass of contradictions maddeningly appealing.

He nodded. "I have call-in-time for parents from seven until seven-thirty, office hours at nine and paperwork in between, unless there's an emergency," he finished, almost smiling again.

Paul picked up a stack of manila folders, which, she could see, were labeled with the names of her family.

"From Dan's files. I had a heck of a time coming up with yours. Do you want it still listed under *Scofield*?"

He knows my entire life story, and he's letting me know bit by bit, she thought.

"I would appreciate it if Dr. Cohen would change it back to Chandler" was the answer she gave him while she tried to look indignant despite the bloodstains, bare feet and bandages.

"I thought so." He opened her file, made a notation and then turned to his prescription pad. "You'll need something for the rest of the day and tonight. By tomorrow aspirin should be enough."

Bay shook her curls. "No, thank you. I'll be fine; I don't need prescription painkillers."

The blue eyes watched her patiently. "Suit yourself, but you have a very low threshold for pain, as this session just indicated. I'm fresh out of bullets and rawhide to bite. Medicine has come a long way, you know; there's no sense in sitting around being miserable."

Was that a reference to her personal life? Her eyes narrowed.

"Whatever you decide, keep your hand dry and use it as little as possible for ten days. No stress, and if you do take the medication, lay off the champagne."

She pulled herself up straight. "I don't usually—"

"No," he broke in, "I'm sure you don't. Anyway, see me in ten days to have the sutures removed."

"I'd prefer Dr. Cohen."

"Dan's on vacation for the month. If you insist, you can see one of the internists covering for him. They're all in Plymouth."

Doctor to patient, the session had come to a close. Blue eyes looked into green. She blinked. "Please have your receptionist bill me."

"Of course."

Paul walked Bay through the neatly piled toys, past the stack of house magazines and children's books in the waiting room. His fingers on her bare arm brought her around, and when he spoke, his voice had the low timbre she had not heard since the terrace Saturday night.

Intimately, nearly at her ear, he sighed then said, "Get some breakfast, preferably a big one, especially if you decide to take the medication. You could use a few pounds, anyway."

"Stay with me," he could have been saying, and for a moment that was all Bay heard. "Stay with me."

"Yes," she stammered, "yes, I will."

His fingers left her arm, and he held open the door. "I must have said something right. That's the healthiest I've seen you look all day."

The color was back, spotting her cheeks. "Thank you for being there" was all she managed to say. "I don't know what I would have done." She left him, and the screen door was empty when she looked up before getting back into the Triumph.

Love-starved sailor nearly bleeds to death before being yanked from jaws of death by gorgeous physician. A physician who thinks his patient was slumming and who makes it painfully clear that he knows every crummy detail of her recently disheveled life.

Three

——

The rest of the day fared no better. It was not that she deliberately intended to ignore the advice of Paul Bendette; it was just that the Midsummer Series started on Sunday, five days away. If she forfeited a whole day, which meant two races, there would be no hope of a decent place in the standings.

Bay intended to finish far more than decently. She intended to win. It was, after all, the one thing at which she excelled.

By nine o'clock that morning she had gotten from the pediatrician's office back to the boathouse and changed out of the ruined T-shirt and shorts and into a sundress. Appropriate, she thought, for a quick trip to the yacht club to register for the races.

The dress was crisp and fresh in direct contrast to the rest of her. Bay's auburn curls had been subjected to the open ride from Newport, saltwater, dusty driveways and traces of blood. In fact, all of her could have done with a good sudsing that suddenly, though not impossible, seemed to be a major undertaking.

She left the boathouse for the second time, her hand numb enough to withstand the pressure of Jeremy's gear shift. Bay found that if she kept a smooth pace and shifted with the tips of her fingers, the maneuver was manageable—just.

Alden's Cove Yacht Club had changed little in the five years since she'd used it actively. The waterfront clubhouse was still white, cavernous and spare: old money. The wicker in the lounge had new chintz cabbage roses, and the secretary had changed her hairstyle. Neither was much of an improvement.

None of the St. Thomas razzmatazz here, Bay thought, a little sorry that she hadn't worn another of her T-shirts just to liven things up.

The secretary registered polite interest in the fact that Bay was back and noted that the Flying Scot was being captained by *Chandler*, not *Scofield*.

"And the name of your crew?"

Bay hedged. "I'm not sure yet.... Can you just assume there will be one by Sunday?"

"Of course," the woman replied. "Just let us know."

Bay said she would, pressing the injured hand against her ribs in an effort to stem the pain as the novocaine wore off. It was beginning to throb painfully again. Nevertheless, she managed to make out a notice for the ACYC bulletin board, hoping an athletic teenager would reply. One who sailed like a champ and took orders well would be ideal.

Fat chance, she told herself, looking at the gauze. She left the clubhouse, barely glancing at the plaque-lined walls peppered with her family's name. The Chandlers had been commodores and champions in categories from the children's "bugs" to the adults' cruising yachts. Sailing was the one category in which Bay hadn't ever let anybody down.

As she lowered herself back into the Triumph, she fished Paul Bendette's prescription from her purse. He had been right, as usual. She needed it.

What she didn't need was the fish-eye from the Alden's Cove pharmacist. Leonard Hooker peered over his counter in surprise.

"Well, Bay Scofield, back for a visit?"

She nodded, handing over the prescription and holding up the injured hand. There was considerable clucking and raising of eyebrows as he read the physician's scrawl.

"Says Whitney Bay Chandler."

"Yes, I know. I'm divorced."

Scrutiny. "Yer folks never mentioned it," he replied.

How tasteful of them, not that it's any of your business. Out loud she simply said, "No?"

He typed the label. "Went to see Bendette?"

"Yes," she answered, "Dr. Cohen's on vacation."

"So he is." The familiar eyes peered over the bifocals. "Set up quite a stir, he did. Had those young mothers lined up around the block when he hung out his shingle with Dan."

"I'm sure Paul Bendette is an excellent physician." She was thinking that he was an excellent dancer and trying to ignore the memory of his arms around her on Saturday night, not to mention his soothing fingers that very morning.

Mr. Hooker handed her the elixir of codeine with an expression that said clearly he was entitled to a few more tidbits.

Bay gave him only her brightest smile, added gauze and adhesive tape to the order and left the shop. *Bay Chandler's back in town.* She might as well have tied a printed streamer to the tail of a plane and flown it over the beach.

She went home immediately and swallowed the dose called for, a teaspoonful that she measured carelessly into a tablespoon. Her stomach held little more than a bowl of dry cereal, and within twenty minutes she was nauseated. It gave her something to concentrate on rather than the pain in her hand that, she had to admit, was fading.

In an effort not to throw up, she slept, falling into deep codeine-induced dreams about floating nursery figures, Leonard Hooker and poisoned apples, bullets between her teeth and princesses. She did not dream about Paul Bendette.

In four hours when the medication had worn off, she decided that the pain was better than nausea. She was filled with empathy for those who lived with constant discomfort. It ate away at her even temperament and made the simplest tasks difficult.

At six she managed to scramble some eggs and butter a muffin, eating her supper on the east-facing balcony. The bay, still dotted with sails, was alive with the slivers of a low sun, still hot on the longest days of the year.

She had gotten herself out of the sundress and into a T-shirt in which she would sleep. A small map of St. Thomas rose and fell over her heart. Had she been better endowed, it would have swelled into cleavage, but instead the small island sat demurely next to the purple script that said Fall in Love with a Virgin over her right breast and St. Thomas over her left.

Clad in the shirt and bikini underpants only, her feet propped on the railing, she was sitting in her canvas-backed director's chair, engrossed in the view, when Paul Bendette's blond head suddenly appeared on the staircase. Bay stood up so fast the chair tipped over, leaving her wide eyed, her injured hand fluttering in the vicinity of the island on her breast.

Paul read the message, smiled at her physical response and turned tactfully to the sea. He was in a suit.

Bay picked up the chair, and when Paul turned back around, she was standing behind it.

"I thought house calls went out with the horse and buggy."

"This one was unexpected," he said as his smile faded.

"You're not kidding. I didn't hear your car."

He was still watching her. His bloodstained shirt had been exchanged for a clean one, and he looked now, at six-thirty, as crisp as he had at dawn.

Paul explained that he'd gotten a flat tire on the compound's gravel weeks before. "I'm still driving on the spare, so I parked at your parents' and walked down."

Bay blinked, trying to think of something intelligent to say about tires. Paul Bendette's physical presence overwhelmed her, and she couldn't think very clearly. Finally she said, "Well, Doctor, I think I'd better go to put something more appropriate on."

Paul was taking off his jacket. "I kind of like you the way you are."

So that was it. Of course, he was here to finish what she'd started last Saturday night. Oh, God. She went through the sliding doors to her bedroom and returned in a man-size terry robe that flaunted her ex-husband's monogram on the pocket. That ought to do it. When she got back, Paul was holding the still-full prescription bottle that she'd left out on the terrace in case she changed her mind about the pain versus nausea.

"You haven't been taking it," he said flatly.

"I know. It makes me sick."

"You should have eaten something. You must be in pain." There was anger now and concern knit into his expression. He put his hands on her shoulders, easing her into the chair.

Bay glared at him. "My hand doesn't hurt that badly and whatever I decide to do about following your instructions in the privacy of my own house is none of your business."

He stared her down. "You're my patient, and there's no one here to keep an eye on you."

"I certainly do not need anyone to keep an eye on me." She shoved herself forward, intending to get up, but hit the table, knocking a glass off onto the deck.

"That remains to be seen."

"Look, Paul—I only took one dose, and that was at noon. It made me nauseous—I certainly wasn't going to take any more. At least give me credit for some common sense!"

Paul sighed, and his fingers widened the knot of his tie. "In the first hour I knew you were alive, I watched you dance barefooted, I dragged you from the edge of a cliff and found myself at the receiving end of a very convincing femme-fatale routine." He seemed pleased that she was blushing.

"Just when I think you are a figment of my imagination—some sprite come and gone in the night—you stagger into my office dressed like something out of *Annie*, faint in my arms over a slice from a bread knife and get blood all over my shirt." He took a breath while she looked at her bare feet. "Forgive me, Whitney or Bay, Robson, Chandler or Scofield . . . a lot of things have been evident, but common sense has yet to be one of them."

The lecture would have been a tirade had he not tempered it with his soothing voice. It was tinged with a weariness but was deep and steady. Calming, she thought. It was getting easier to imagine him stilling fears in children.

"It's Bay," she replied, "Bay Chandler."

His gaze dropped to the gauzed hand she cradled in her strong one.

"Bay, you should have called me when the medication reacted. We could have cut the dosage, or I could have prescribed something else." His eyes came back to hers.

Her lashes lowered. "Maybe I do need a doctor."

"I'm not here as one, that is, I wasn't intending to be. We have unfinished business—"

Her eyes flew open. "Paul, I know what you must think, the way I behaved . . . I'm sure I led you to believe that I wanted to take things, uh, further, but—"

"But what?" he interrupted. "As long as I was just part of Sea Mist's staff, it was okay? After all, you weren't likely to run into a security guard again, were you?"

The pain that showed in Bay's face was not caused by her hand. "No! That's not it at all."

"Isn't it? Weren't you delighted to have been 'out being seduced by the hired help'?"

Bay's left hand flew over her mouth. "Jeremy!"

Paul leaned back against the railing, his ankles crossed, his arms crossed, too, until he loosened the tie further then removed it and then his tan suit jacket. She wanted to tell him to keep his clothes on.

"I saw your brother the next morning. When he found out I'd been at the dance, he couldn't wait to tell me about you, what a shame it was I'd missed finally meeting the mysterious sailing sister from St. Thomas.

"Seems little sis was having the time of her life, though, dancing in the moonlight with the grandson of the servants."

"And you told him everything?" She looked at the sisal mat, wondering if she should crawl under it.

"Not a word. I wasn't entirely sure you were who you are, or if you meant me, for that matter. Not until this morning." He shook his head. "Hard to believe the waif on my examining table was the same—"

"You've made your point. You've come to humiliate me and now you have, but that's as far as it goes. I've come home from the islands to be alone, contrary to my behavior Saturday night. I'd had too much to drink and too much advice from that cretin of a brother." She cleared her throat, pleased that at least she had taken charge. "I want to be alone."

"Greta Garbo was more convincing" was all he said. He was still leaning against the railing, but now he started rolling up his shirt sleeves. She wished his arms weren't so tanned. Forearms didn't usually produce a reaction in her diaphragm.

"Whitney Bay, you're in pain and you're in no condition to be alone whether you want to be or not."

"That's ridiculous." She walked the length of the deck but on the way back, the terry tie, which she had fumbled with earlier, fell from her waist to the flooring. Without thinking, she lowered her right hand for it as the robe fell open, and she gasped in pain. He was beside her in an instant, letting her support the throbbing hand with her strong fingers.

"You want me to do you back up?"

"No! That is, yes. But don't touch me!"

He lifted the strip of fabric. "I'll see if I can restrain myself." She stood still, feeling like a total fool, knowing she looked like death warmed over, embarrassed to the roots of her hair that she could have thought he'd come for anything intimate.

In another moment he had layered one side of the robe inside the other, pressed warm, professional fingers across her stomach to do so and neatly tied the sash. "Forgive me," he said with more than a touch of sarcasm.

"My instructions," he continued as if nothing had happened, "were for you to keep that hand immobile. Ten days, as a matter of fact. I've just come from the yacht club. Went down to sign up for the Flying Scot Series."

"Oh," she said in a small voice.

"You have no business racing on Sunday."

"But what were you doing at the yacht club? Here I thought you were so proud of your working-class roots," she replied.

"Don't change the subject. My instructions were to use your hand as little as possible for ten days."

"Yes, you just said that. I promise not to sue if the sutures rip."

He shook his head. "I've seen to that. I signed on as your crew. I might as well tell you now that I intend to do the sailing, however."

"What? You can't crew for me. I won't have you as crew!"

"It's done. We working-class types can be very persuasive."

"I can't believe this. I can't believe you'd want to be a member of the club for that matter."

He shrugged. "Social contacts are great for business. And with the M.D. after my name, they didn't seem to object."

She was biting her lip to keep down the rage and laughter, a combination that made her feel as though she were full of half-a-dozen gin and tonics.

"Stop looking so damned smug. I may have needed a doctor this morning, but I do not need one in my boat. I want a sailor and I intend to find one. One who takes orders. This is *my* life!"

They stood face to face in the dimming light as the sun fell behind the boathouse. The fire in Bay's eyes could have lighted the apartment.

"Would you like a lecture on permanent damage to your thumb? Draining infections that have reached the tendons?"

"No."

"Perhaps it would soothe your ruffled feathers if I told you that I am an excellent sailor. I've even been known to give Breck Scofield a run for his money."

"Breck?" She looked at the monogram on her pocket.

"I'm a Newport townie. I never sailed for the clubs, but we faced off for years in the town regattas."

"And I'm supposed to be delighted at this piece of news? Do you know how irritating it is that you keep dropping little pieces of information like crumbs under my nose? I hate it! Stop it!"

"I wasn't aware that you were still sensitive about your ex-husband."

"That's not what's bothering me."

Paul turned back to the view, the one that wasn't in terry cloth. "If you had any sense at all, Bay, you'd be thrilled to crew for me."

"I have no sense. Saturday night proved that. And, Paul Bendette, I am not crewing for you. I'm sailing my own boat, myself."

"Well, for your own medical safety, you had better accept the fact that Sunday you are crewing for me, even if it's in your boat." He looked pleased and thoughtful then said suddenly, "Why did you marry him?"

Bay had a headache and a grinding pain in her wrist. She sank her forehead into her good palm. "Because it seemed like a good idea at the time. I have very questionable taste in men." Stop looking at me, she wanted to scream. Stop looking into my soul as though it had a window.

She started to work at getting the conversation back on track. "If you're as good a crew as you say, Paul, you're wasting your time with me. I would much rather sail against you so I can beat the pants off you." She heard herself say it and then fumbled for words to clarify her meaning. "I meant that figuratively."

He grinned. "I'm sure you did. And after the series? After the summer?"

"I still want your pants on." This time she laughed, but he was silent, probably waiting for her to get serious. "I don't know. I came home to be by myself, sort things out." She ran her hand over the back of the canvas chair. "I'm not as goal oriented as you."

"Being goal oriented got me out."

"Out," she repeated, "is an interesting choice of words. Were things so bad?"

"No. I just wanted more."

"To go back to the old neighborhood and have everyone call you 'Doctor'?" Pain gave her amazing audacity.

Paul's expression changed. "I suppose you'd think that. No, the truth is I wanted to study medicine as far back as I can remember. It was a goal I aimed for and got."

"Blood, sweat and tears," she replied.

"You, Bay Chandler, will never know the half of it."

She looked at him fully, afraid of just how much she did want to know about him. She was usually so good at maintaining distance, even flirting she had honed to a fine, impersonal skill. It took her a moment to shift her gaze.

"And you, Bay. What do you want?"

Oh, no you don't. She looked out into the horizon. "Clean hair, that's what I want. Clean everything." She looked at her hand with renewed disgust.

"I can give you that."

Her heart thumped under the map. She laughed politely. "Right."

"I'm a physician," he added, as if that would change her mind.

"And I'm a sailor. You're also a man."

"Suit yourself. If you prefer wrapping your hand in a Baggie and sticking your head under the faucet, go right ahead."

Somehow she had expected more determined persuasion. "You'd wash my hair and—behave yourself? What if I drive you wild with desire?"

He laughed. It was rich and genuine and full of affection. "I'm thirty-four years old, and I think I can probably keep myself under control. Heaven knows in that getup it will be hell, however."

She laughed, too. "I look terrible, don't I?"

He brushed her hair. "Let's just say it's not like last Saturday night."

"I must be out of my mind." She was returning his look.

"I've thought so for five days now," Paul said, turning to weave his way between the sliding doors and make for her living room.

Once inside, he complimented her on the decor and then led the way to the bathroom, which separated the bedroom from where they stood. With a twist to the faucet, he started running the water.

"Paul, I thought we were talking about my hair."

"Wanna live a little?"

She thought of St. Thomas, the loose, easygoing lifestyle, the countless moonlight dips with friends, charterers. At that moment the thought of sinking into a warm, soothing tub and being scrubbed clean was temptation itself. She nodded and undid the robe. "Turn around."

To her surprise, he did. She kicked off the panties and yanked the T-shirt over her head with one hand. When she was finally naked, she took a hand towel and pressed it to her body and stepped into the water. "Okay, Doc. The shampoo's in the vanity drawer."

He reached for it and the cup from the sink. "Head back."

Bay closed her eyes, letting the warm water run through her hair, feeling the cold globs of shampoo as he squeezed the bottle, and then his fingers moving through her curls. She thought her bones would melt.

"Hand still hurt a lot?"

Ah, conversation. "To tell you the truth, once we started arguing, I forgot about it. It's much better." All of that came out as a croaky whisper while Paul worked the lather with slow, deliberate strokes along her temples and the nape of her neck. The grip of her gauzed fingers on the soap dish handle was the only thing keeping her upright.

"Head back."

She obeyed and he rinsed, then rinsed again. Before she knew it, soapy hands were running over her shoulders and down her spine. Behind her there was a moan, and a washcloth fell onto her knees. "You had better soap yourself," he said. "Restraint is becoming a major undertaking."

With her back to him she smiled, feeling nothing but pleasure at the sound of his tight voice.

Bay did as she was told in comfortable silence, knowing Paul was having as much trouble as she was. He unplugged the drain then got up, pulling the bath towel from its rack and standing with it stretched between his arms.

Bay smiled self-consciously and dropped the soaking hand towel she'd been holding in front of her and let him wrap her in the fresh terry. His fingers lingered on her shoulders. She thought he might have to hold her up.

"Thank you, Paul," she said in a whisper.

"My pleasure." She could see that it was. "There's more," he added when she was all wrapped up.

Her eyes widened. "Oh, I don't think so."

He smiled. "A hair dryer is what I had in mind, and I'll change the dressing for good measure."

And then you and I can go somewhere and live happily ever after, Prince Charming. Bay cleared her throat for the fourth time. She was warm, relaxed and off her guard. He didn't look treacherous, this goal oriented baby doctor.

While he plugged in the dryer, she looked at the tiny heap of T-shirt and panties, wondering how she would get back into them discreetly. Paul was probably thinking of ways to keep her out of them discreetly.

Nevertheless, he flicked the switch, and she sat on the stool, letting him run his fingers through her hair until it fluffed into mounds of clean curls.

"You remind me of a spaniel I once had," he said over the blower. So much for treachery. The chance to dress discreetly came when the pager on his belt beeped. He went through the door when she gestured to the phone next to her bed.

Bay wiggled back into the clothes, listening to him talk with his answering service, his voice low, authoritative, as he had been with her that morning. A voice she had trusted with her life. Something even deeper than her heart stirred and pulled away.

She left the towels and joined him. Paul smiled that smile and patted the spread. "You, Cinderella, are adorable."

"Paul!" She flushed, pleased and confused.

"Adorable gorgeous, adorable bloodsoaked, adorable wet and adorable dry."

"Flattery will get you everywhere."

"Not tonight." He looked at his watch. "Get into bed. I'll change the dressing, tuck you in and be on my way."

"You're leaving?"

"You want me to stay?"

She stammered and pulled back the spread. "No. No, I don't. Although I appreciate everything you've done. The children of this town are lucky to have you." She was surprised to hear herself say it and touched by the expression on his face as he, the physician again, raised his hand to the side of her face.

He simply said "Thank you" and then went back to the vanity for the bandages. Three minutes later she sat under the sheet in her T-shirt with Paul on the edge of the bed. He methodically changed the dressing in a way that was sensual and stimulating and yet completely professional. She sat there, leaning against the pillows fighting her attraction to him. It was a good thing he didn't take her pulse.

Instinctively she pulled the sheet up over her breasts, a ridiculous gesture, considering the man had already pressed a stethoscope there—not to mention the bath. He continued to concentrate on her hand, looking closely at the repair.

"I do good work."

It made her laugh.

"Still hurt?"

"A little," she said, and caught a look of compassion on his face, as if he would have pulled the pain into himself if he could have.

"Is it manageable?"

She nodded. "Maybe an aspirin or two..."

He rose and got them, along with a glass of water, then rewrapped the wound. She had never considered knuckles erotic, but given half a chance, she could have fallen in love with his. She shifted her toes, and the sheet slid down. Paul smiled at her again.

"You make for very interesting reading."

"Yes," she answered, "but the library's closed for the evening."

"Just as well. I have another patient to check on." The fresh gauze was on her hand and the adhesive tape in place. He stood up. "Of course, they don't all get this kind of treatment."

"I should hope not," she said, pleased that he smiled again.

"This particular patient is a new mother whose three-month-old has recurrent ear infections. Nothing too serious yet, but she had lost her first—miscarried—and she's still shaky."

There was one violent lurch behind Bay's breast-bone, a searing ache and then nothing. She nodded. "Well then, you'd better go. Thanks for all of this. I feel clean and relaxed and pampered, to tell you the truth."

"Good," he whispered, bending down to her. She closed her eyes as the crown of his hay-colored hair brushed her cheek and he found her lips. It was a light kiss, and she had to fight to keep from tangling her arms around his neck.

"Get some sleep, Captain," he said softly, pulling away.

"Yes," she murmured, "I will, sailor."

He let himself out through the sliding doors in the bedroom, and she listened to his footsteps on the deck, the gravel and finally to the distant engine of his car.

Four

———

Following the doctor's orders was not difficult since Bay had no plans. She stayed at home, lolling on her balcony, scanning the harbor and trying not to think about a relationship that would be impossible.

"Impossible" was what she was saying at two when the phone rang. She was sunbathing in the nude and exchanged her iced tea for the receiver. Helen Day, the Alden's Cove Yacht Club secretary, was confirming the fact that Jean-Paul Bendette, M.D., was now registered as crew.

She should have told Helen to take his name off the list, but the chances of finding someone with the few days left were risky at best. He *had* said he was an excellent sailor, she thought, someone in Breck Scofield's league.

The phone rang again. "Are you following my instructions?"

Her immediate response to Paul's voice made Bay reach for a towel. She cleared her throat. "To the letter," she replied. "I am immobile, every inch of me."

There was a soft laugh. "And the wound?"

"Nearly pain free."

"Good," he said, still sounding crisp and professional. "It occurred to me that we'd be wasting all that perfectly clean skin and hair if we didn't get you out of that boathouse. I have a standing reservation at Wingate's Galley on Wednesday nights. How about it?"

She needed an excuse. "I don't think so, Paul." She was pulling back again, and she could tell by the silence on the phone that her refusal was unexpected. This was not a man used to being turned down, she knew. Especially when she had let him...well, they *had* kissed. She tried not to think about the bath. "I wouldn't be able to cut my meat."

"I have the skill of a surgeon," he said and then he laughed, and the sound permeated her like the sun. She agreed and hung up, as troubled by her physical response to him as she was intrigued by it. She had come home to think, to sort out her life, to be alone. She was even failing at that.

She wiggled herself into a sundress banded across the bodice by elastic. It was flattering even without the addition of paper tissue, and best of all there were no buttons or ties. Paul arrived promptly at seven and gave her a frown.

"I was hoping you'd need some assistance."

She shook her curls. "I'm very independent."

"Heaven knows you work hard enough at it," he said, lifting the tumbler of clear red liquid she had offered.

Bay smiled. "Cranberry juice. Scout's honor."

Paul's blond eyebrows arched. "You were never a Girl Scout. It would have taken an entire troop to keep up with you."

She laughed, letting the breeze blow the cotton against her bare legs, aware of how relaxed she was in his presence. She looked from her own drink to his blue eyes. "I am capable of behaving myself. You've only seen me full of liquor or full of pain, Paul. There's a woman under all of that you hardly know."

That was hardly true. He'd been letting her know since she'd fainted in his arms that he knew far more about her than she would have guessed—or ever intended to tell so early in a relationship.

Paul watched the boats on the water, and Bay watched Paul. He was dressed simply, the first time she'd seen him in khakis and a polo shirt. If anything, he was even handsomer when he was a little ruffled than in a suit or evening clothes.

"What does your father do?" she asked, not caring in the least, but wanting to balance this a little more in her favor.

He turned and studied her for an instant. "He worked for the Navy Yard before they pulled out and then ran a body shop. Damned good mechanic. So was my grandfather, of course."

Bay sipped. "You come by your tinkering naturally, I guess. How about your mother?"

"Keeps the books for Dad and raised six of us." Paul's response was studied, tempered by watching her.

Bay unconsciously pressed the gauzed hand to her cheek.

"You must be very proud of them," she said, and when he didn't reply, she looked back at him. "Have I said something wrong?"

His blond head moved back and forth. "No, of course not. It's just that in this neck of the woods I usually hear how proud they must be of me. I think your social strata envision my life as one long climb from poverty."

Bay dismissed it with a snort. "I wouldn't think learning what makes people tick is that far removed from what makes engines tick. Sort of a natural progression, in your case, from two generations of men and machines."

Paul put down the empty glass. "You are amazing, you know that?"

She grinned. "Yes. Also starving." It would have been lovely now to touch him. She wanted to brush his shoulder or find a loose thread to pull from his shirt. One of six children, happy family...he was taking on three dimensions. She never should have asked.

They filled the time it took to travel the distance between the boathouse and the restaurant with safe topics: the improvement in her hand, Paul's knowledge of racing, the upcoming series. And with not-so-safe topics: the fact that she wasn't in Bermuda with the rest of her family, the deserted beach for which she was named and whether either of them would take commands well during the race.

"You're to sit still on Sunday," he said in the parking lot.

"Impossible," she said then turned as somebody called her name, her previous one, that is.

"Bay Scofield?" The call came again, and she focused on an approaching couple, who were all smiles. The woman was a contemporary, a friend from what seemed another life. She looked from Bay to Paul and back. "Are you and Breck back for the summer? Don't tell me you two managed to have babies *and* lead the most romantic life—"

"I'm back. Breck and I have been divorced for two years." Whatever appetite she had had, it disappeared. There was an awkward silence, and then Bay touched the woman's arm. "Doesn't bother me, don't let it bother you. No children, either." Her throat hurt. "I met Dr. Bendette over my own emergency."

Paul finished the conversation with his usual breeziness after he had been introduced to the husband. They stood, one couple behind the other, waiting to be shown to their tables. Bay concentrated on the view, which included her family's sail lofts, and draggers chugging back to the harbor after a full day's fishing.

While they waited and on their way to the table, Paul was also greeted by several couples and hugged around the knees by a four-year-old. Bay felt like a goldfish, pressed up against the edge of an aquarium. Needless to say, once they were seated, their mood was subdued. "You do have your public," she said over the salad.

"Children and spaniels adore me. I'm working on wild-haired yacht captains."

Bay should have laughed. "It might not be worth the effort."

He lowered his fork. "What the hell is that supposed to mean?"

She didn't know herself, only felt as if someone inside her were erecting a barrier. "I don't know. I didn't expect this—seeing people, making explanations...."

"They seemed genuinely interested in you, Bay. *Your* public."

"Genuinely interested in my dirty laundry."

The main course arrived, flounder, which she cut easily with her fork. Paul was quiet, too, looking at the twinkling lights of the Chandler buildings.

"Did you or Breck ever consider working over there?"

"I used to help out some during summer vacations. My father always hoped Breck would join—to settle him down, I think. It seemed too close to home, back then. Jeremy and Christopher were enough like bodyguards at the compound. I didn't need it nine-to-five, too. Chris is a naval architect, Jeremy's vice president and Dad owns the damn thing. Enough's enough."

"And off you went?"

Bay looked at her dinner companion, his face full of honest concern, ever the doctor.

"Off I went," she answered. "It seemed ideal. I'm a late baby, as they say. I think I wore my parents out. By the time I met Breck and insisted I wanted to spend the rest of my life sailing in the Virgins with him, they were too exhausted to argue." She sipped her coffee and grinned, her first smile since she'd started in on the flounder. "*I* can be very persuasive."

"I've noticed."

The ride home was quiet, bristling with unanswered questions to topics they touched on. Bay felt as though they'd hit every raw nerve in her body. As they passed the Big House, lit by timers, she turned in her seat.

"You seem to be chancing more flat tires, since you've switched back to driving to the boathouse."

Probably you just want to get me home as quickly as possible after my behavior tonight, she thought.

"Just being around you is taking a chance."

The engine died. Out in front of them there was the moon and stars, hanging over the water lapping on the sand. It was all commonplace to Bay, and she took little notice of anything except the knot in her emotions. "What's that supposed to mean?" She knew very well what it was supposed to mean.

"Erratic. You can be open, free, sexy one minute, then bam! You shut yourself up like a clam. I don't know what you're doing half the time."

Neither do I, she thought. "I didn't expect old friends and patients crawling all over us."

His hand brushed the steering wheel. "None of them deserved your behavior."

She got out of the car and marched toward the staircase to her apartment. Paul caught up with her effortlessly, halting her with a light grasp on her arm.

"They didn't, and neither do I."

"Well, I don't deserve to be put under a microscope just because I'm in a public place. I can't stand the thought that this town is gloating over my failure. What a juicy piece of gossip: Bay and Breck, the perfect couple, no longer quite so perfect."

She turned from him, not wanting him upstairs, heading instead for the beach. Paul let her set the pace until the clipped grass gave way to sand.

"You'll ruin another pair of shoes unless you listen to me."

"I don't want to listen to you." Nevertheless, Bay kicked off her espadrilles. Paul kept going until he reached the boulders mounded on the border of the property. He crossed his arms, looking at the kelp and coupling horseshoe crabs, lying like paired army helmets at the waterline.

"Sexy devils," he said when she was next to him.

"I don't want to talk about the mating habits of those ugly things."

"Or any other things?"

He looked right at her, and he appeared shadowy, handsome, disgusted. "Bay Scofield's back in town. She's using her maiden name again. It'll be yesterday's news in a week."

"It's nobody's business. How can you defend them?"

"I didn't see anyone treating it as *business*," he shot back. "They were friends once and they care. No more, no less."

"They seemed very curious about the fact that I was with you."

"Hell, Bay, the last anyone knew you were married and living a fantasy life in the Virgin Islands." His voice, no longer a murmur, was direct and edged with irritation. "Perhaps it hasn't occurred to you that whom I'm seen with in this town is news, too. I've had offers that would make your head spin. A thirty-four-year-old physician in private practice has a certain appeal and dinner invitations through Christmas. Working-class roots or not."

The remark brought Bay's head up sharply, and she caught his glare.

"There are women even willing to overlook my humble beginnings."

"Then why aren't you with one of them now?" She looked away from him into the dark. They were not touching, yet she absorbed his energy and could feel the tension. The desire to be in his arms was as strong as the desire to run.

"Look at me, Bay."

She turned slowly in the sea breeze, pulling in a puff of breath as both his hands steadied her face. "I am where I want to be." Her resistance melted. Like candle wax, warm, pliant, immobile, she stood as he kissed her. And then her arms went around him, pressing him with her good hand and her wrist and her forearms and every other inch that could feel the powerful restraint in him. Her own eagerness terrified her as the pleasure tore at her heart. She wanted it to be Saturday, wanted him, the anonymous stranger, gone before there was time to be foolish.

This man had the ability to strip away pretense, no matter what she tried. He dug at her soul and was far worse than Jeremy and a thousand times more dangerous. There was nothing brotherly about Paul Bendette's intentions. More dangerous still, there was nothing sisterly about hers.

Under the strip of moon, he held her face. "If we hadn't been interrupted at Sea Mist, would you have made love to me?"

She tried to turn her head, closing her eyes against the pressure and the warmth. "Yes," she lied. Stop probing! Stop searching! she commanded silently.

She felt his chest expand. "Because I was the help and that insured nothing more than a one-night stand?"

"Yes," she lied again, hoping it would hurt enough for him to back off. He dropped his hands and turned to the sea.

"And now, Bay?"

She couldn't look at him. "Now I am relieved that I didn't follow my baser instincts." She hoped he'd think that she had the sensitivity of a horseshoe crab or that she was hopelessly scrawny or shiftless. Anything!

"Can you imagine, Paul? Even if I hadn't cut my hand, we'd have met sooner or later. Conniving Jeremy would have us to dinner, and there you'd be, staring at me across the dining room table, thinking 'Now what am I going to do with her!'"

"Yes." He sounded bitter. "It's a great leveler, intimacy. There you'd sit all wit and bravado, like now, across from the hired help who had seen you at your most vulnerable. Across from someone who had shared the moments when you couldn't hide behind your wall, when he might have glimpsed some honesty, even if one night's worth."

She jammed her hands over her ears. "Stop it. Don't you know I'm lying? I wouldn't have done anything Saturday night. It wouldn't have been *love*, it wouldn't have been anything, anything at all. It couldn't be with you, not now." It seemed like the perfect time to run and she did, leaving Paul and her espadrilles, heading for the boathouse.

He, of course, caught up with her as she sank onto the risers, fighting tears and a wave of loneliness more powerful than the guilt for hurting him.

Paul sat down next to her. She hated herself. She wished she could hate him.

They sat in silence on the steps until her breathing slowed, and the tears she willed to stay in her eyes did.

"You're very good at running away, you know that, don't you?"

She nodded.

"Don't do me any favors. Maybe I am out of my league in this one, Bay. Maybe your blood's too blue, and my background's got too much axle grease in it. A little honesty wouldn't hurt, right now. We're both going to have to live in this town, run into each other. Who knows, I may wind up treating *your* children.''

He was putting her heart through a shredder, and two dime-size tears finally escaped, sliding over her cheeks. He looked at her and shook his head. "Come on, Blueblood, I'm the one who's supposed to be all torn up. You're the most complicated woman I've ever run into. Bar none."

"Paul," she choked, pulling her courage from the depths of her depression, "how can you think I give a damn about your background? What on earth do you take me for?"

"I wish to hell I knew."

She bit her lip, almost smiling. "It's not who you are. It's what you are." She stood up. He did, too.

"You'd like me better if I were in livery, driving a limo?"

Oh, Lord. "Forget it. I want to go up. I have a splitting headache, and I think we've said enough for one night."

His warm sturdy fingers came around her arm again. "I think we've danced enough around the issues for one night," he said.

Defeat, she acknowledged. "Why can't your beeper go off now? Don't you have patients with ear infections or strep throats or something? There must be an emergency room you need to visit."

He laughed. "I've got my hands full with an emotional crisis right here, an emergency I'd like to be part of. Bay, Saturday night I was ready to play because I thought you were. Now I'm ready to listen."

"Well, I'm not ready to talk."

He kissed her ear. "Wanna play?"

"I want to be left alone."

"You throw that out a lot. Sorry, sailor, I don't buy it."

"Paul, I'm serious. Saturday was a huge mistake. Can't you see that? All we've done is argue."

"I seem to recall some kissing." His thumbs massaged her collarbone.

"Forget the kissing. I don't want to get involved with you. I can't."

"All right!" The sudden change in him made her jump. "Forget the humor, forget the gentle prying. I quit. You want me gone—I'm not a glutton for punishment, Bay. I'll go. I hope someday, if you can't be honest with me, you'll at least be honest with yourself. And by God, if Breck Scofield has done this to you, he ought to be shot."

Her eyes widened as she watched him leave. It took every ounce of strength she possessed to go after him and not up to the safety of the big brass bed.

She reached him as he opened the car door. "It isn't Breck, not now, not ever. I couldn't keep him, couldn't be what he wanted, couldn't— It isn't Breck, it's me."

Paul stood still, looking at her. She kept going, knowing that in a few more moments she'd lose her nerve, and they'd be back to the awful silences. "It's me. I thought I had it all buried and forgotten until I realized what you are. You won't ever treat my children, because I won't have any. I lost the only thing I ever really wanted."

"Wait a minute, Cinderella—"

"I am not Cinderella, and you're not Prince Charming! And nobody's living happily ever after."

"Damn right," he broke in again. "All this time I've thought it was my background making you put on your brakes. I misread it completely. I am a baby doctor. That's it, isn't it? I'm a constant reminder that you miscarried.''

He had pulled the plug on what was left of her emotions, and she sank against him. ''Jeremy.''

''Bay, darling, Jeremy didn't tell me. It's in your file, documented by Dan after your parents flew you home from Charlotte Amalie. I read it Monday after I sutured your hand. But there was no indication that the trauma was so enormous.''

She was barely listening, wanting to separate herself from further torment but unable to pull away from the comfort. Though her mind still fought him, her body, which had done nothing but betray her since Paul Bendette had walked down the stairs at Sea Mist, molded itself against him. As deep as the ache was for what he had revealed, so was the sense of relief.

He was leaning against the car, and she was leaning against him as he brought her face up. ''It does not mean there won't be more children, and it doesn't mean you've failed. Not Breck, not yourself, not anybody.''

Her throat was tight, the tears millimeters from spilling again. ''I wanted that baby. I would have had someone to love me, even now.''

''I love you,'' he whispered, ''if you'll only let me.''

Five

It was useless to tell him this was not what she wanted. Before the words formed in her brain, her lips were captured, parting on their own to welcome the man who knew her better than she knew herself.

It would not be enough, of course, deep kisses on a Wednesday night under the moon, but it would have to do. She drew back, sighing.

"Temptation," he growled into her hair, holding her in a hug.

"I think we've said enough for tonight."

He kissed her neck. "The barriers are down, Bay. There's no need for them to go up again."

She moved her head in a partial nod, rubbing her hair against him as he nuzzled her and then let her go. "I think maybe you've taken the first step in resolving some of the garbage you've been carrying around, too."

"Garbage. Is that a medical term?"

"Yup. It describes perfectly what happens to feelings and issues that don't get resolved."

"And I suppose you see yourself as the one to help resolve?"

"Of course. I knew the moment I saw you trying to throw yourself off Cliff Walk that what you needed was a tall blond physician who sails like the wind."

"Or takes the wind out of my sails?" she whispered.

He kissed the bridge of her nose. "You play a great game, letting the world think you don't care about anything. I think life's taken the wind out your sails, Blueblood. I want you to see yourself as I do."

"Which is?"

"Perfection."

Her heart leaped. "Oh, Paul, I'm so far from that."

He was smiling. "How would you know? You haven't even gotten to know yourself." He drew her back into his arms and kissed her until she was weak from wanting him. Physical attraction was so easy. She didn't have to think, she just had to feel.

Those feelings, however, were threatening to overwhelm her. She pulled back with a deep sigh.

"What will you do tomorrow?" Paul asked.

"Nurse my hand and stare at the phone until it rings."

He smiled. "Am I being led to believe I'm making progress?"

"I think both of us are."

When the phone's jangling shattered her sleep, Bay opened her eyes to another perfect day. "Hello?"

"I wouldn't want you to pine away a day this gorgeous by staring at the phone."

She smiled and sat up. "What makes you think I meant I wanted *you* to call?"

"I think it had something to do with the way you ran your fingers through my hair. Doctors know these things."

"Do they? How perceptive."

"Yes," he replied. "The body doesn't lie."

"Whose?" she asked, nestling into the pillows.

"Ours," he said in a whisper.

"Goodness, is this an obscene phone call?"

There was the incredible, sensual laugh. "Only if you want it to be, but I have a better idea. How about a quick sail about five-thirty tonight? I have to be at the hospital at eight, but I can squeeze you in."

"That sounds lovely, especially the squeezing part." How easy it was to flirt. "I'll throw together some supper, too."

"Good. Then it's a date."

"Yes." She paused. "By the way, who is this?"

There was a growl, a low laugh and a mumbled obscenity.

"Paul Bendette," she said. "I thought so."

She replaced the receiver and gave some thought to what she could do to kill the next ten hours. She didn't manage to kill the day by thinking about her miscarriage, but it certainly killed the mood. Paul's ability to grapple with her torment—to make her grapple with it—raised long-aching memories to the surface.

But the pain was balanced by anticipation, and the more she thought about what caused her melancholy, the more she thought about the man who seemed so willing to help her face it. Did love come so easily to Paul Bendette that he knew what he felt for her in less time than it would have taken Bay to chart a cruise?

Had he been in love before? Risked it? Had time for it? Was she so transparent that he knew how ready she was, how she ached to find what she thought she'd lost? And what on earth made her think the answer lay in someone who would be a constant reminder of her failures? Someone so handsome he lit up Newport even in a rented penguin suit.

She contemplated all of this while making a pasta salad and also when she went shopping for an armload of clothes. She wandered the shops in the village, avoiding familiar faces, thinking how Paul would want her to march right up and shake long-forgotten hands. It had been a long time since she thought about what someone else wanted her to do.

Not that coming home had been entirely her own idea. Jeremy and Christopher had threatened to come and kidnap her if she didn't give herself a summer "where she belonged."

Maybe she belonged. It remained to be seen.

At four-fifteen with forty-five minutes until Paul's arrival, she dressed laboriously, damning her hand. Everything she did was laborious. Ten days. She shook her head.

Finally, dressed in a pink rugby shirt and shorts, Topsiders, her hair none too clean, her palms began to sweat in anticipation.

At five she sat on the director's chair, her feet up on the rail, watching the boats. She studied the distant gaff rig of a catboat until it was out of sight and then contemplated her cuticles. She wasn't a nail biter, but she gave it serious thought. At five-fifteen she studied the grommets in her boat shoes and at five-thirty she made herself a gin and tonic, mostly tonic.

At six o'clock she was grateful dinner wasn't to be served hot, and at six-thirty she tried to convince herself that Paul Bendette was not worth the mental torment she had suffered through for the past twelve hours.

At six-thirty the physician climbed her stairs, his voice preceding him. "'I must go down to the seas again, to the vagrant gypsy life, To the gull's way and the whale's way, where the wind's like a whetted knife....'" He grinned at her. "Hi, Blueblood. Ready?"

She did nothing to mask her astonishment. "Ready! You arrive as if you're on time, quoting John Masefield—"

He raised his index finger. "Bad form to mention to a pediatrician that he's an hour-and-a-half late."

"And it's not bad form to *be* late?" She put her hands on her hips. "Sick children come first? You just said you wanted the vagrant gypsy life."

He took her drink from the table and managed a large swallow.

"There's gin in it," she said.

He handed it back. "The bad news is that I'm very late. The good news is that I'm yours for the evening. Got the night off at the last minute. Meeting was canceled."

Her heart jumped. Hers for the evening?

He continued to quote, "'All I ask is a merry yarn from a laughing fellow rover...'" and then he cupped her head while he finished the poem. "'And a quiet sleep and a sweet dream when the long *trek's* over.'"

Bay's lower lip tingled. "John Masefield said that?"

"Mmm," he said while he kissed her mouth. He was still cold from the ice cubes and he tasted fizzy, like tonic and citrus. It was delicious.

When she came down off her tiptoes, she suggested that they head for the yacht club.

"We're losing our daylight, Doc."

He acquiesced and within half an hour they were in the club's launch, which taxied them from the pier to the Chandler Flying Scot. The twenty-one-foot boat was rigged, its triangular sail lowered and fastened to the boom. The sloop rig also carried a smaller jib, and for the downwind leg of the races, a spinnaker to balloon out in front of the bow.

The Scots, a popular fleet in the Cove, were all moored in the same area, and as they thanked the launch driver and boarded Bay's, she looked to where Paul indicated his boat was. "You may regret not using it," she said.

"If I were to use it, you'd regret it."

She grinned. "Because of injuring my hand, of course. You'd never beat me, Townie."

He raised the sail, enforcing his demand that she do nothing but "look adorable."

The triangular course, set with buoys in the bay, was deserted now, though the wind was still stiff for such a late hour. What started as an evening cruise worked itself into a demonstration of skill and expertise. Bay finally insisted on working the tiller with her good hand, and while she steered them, Paul took the sheets, adjusting both jib and mainsail to the fullest advantage.

They didn't begin to argue until he refused to let her do anything else. "We don't have enough daylight to run the spinnaker leg, anyway," he said.

"I feel like ballast," she complained.

He was watching the sail for luffing, already concentrating, hardly hearing her. "Forget it. On Sunday I can handle this fine with you hiking. By the next race the sutures will be out."

It was useless to argue. She knew she'd just do what she thought would make them win, regardless. Bay followed his gaze. "Head off."

"What?" he said.

"Head off. You're too close to the wind—I'll take the sheet myself. You take the tiller."

"No way!" He let the sheet out a breath, and the nylon filled, pulling the Scot, making her heel at her most efficient.

"Atta boy!"

He glared at her. "I meant what I said about permanent injury. It's one lousy day. You can behave for that long, can't you? There's a lot you *can* do, just weighting the boat and bossing me around."

Bay laughed. "You always do that, you know…make me laugh when I'm irritated as hell."

He grinned at her. "What choice do I have? You don't quit. It may be choppy out here Sunday, and I might refuse to let you on board for all you know."

"This is my boat!"

"I happen to know that this is Jeremy's boat. He bought it in seventy-nine, when your father added Scot sails to their line."

"Is there anything you don't know about us?" she sighed.

He looked again at the mast, his hair blown from his face, his eyes gleaming in the evening light. It was a face full of maturity and the compassion his profession required, the touchstone of his character. Not for the first time, something deep inside her stirred then ached, something underneath the banter about sailing and the silliness of playing boss.

When he turned to her, she looked at the horizon. "There's not much I don't know. I met your brother when I bought sails for my own Scot. That was before I knew what a crazy little sister he had."

"Kept me a secret, did he?" She moved the tiller to avoid a lobster buoy.

"Not for long. I came within a hair of chartering you and your boat last winter."

Her eyebrows arched. "What changed your mind?"

He laughed. "The desire to eat for the rest of the year. I couldn't possibly afford your rates *and* my rent and my need for food three times a day."

Bay was enjoying herself thoroughly. "What'd you do instead?"

"Stayed with my sister in Burlington, Vermont, and skied Stowe for four days. Even that barely left me grocery money."

She smiled at him, knowing that joking aside, money was a problem, and had probably been even more of one until his practice had been established. He didn't seem to mind her curiosity. They changed tack, came about sharply at the first mark and headed back toward the mooring in the dying light. Cruising was a lot more sociable than racing. Sunday there would be little conversation.

"Six kids," she said. "How did you manage college and med school?"

"We're a regular Walton family. My brothers are in business with my father, and they helped. Scholarships, loans, jobs, you name it."

"I will," she quipped. "Let's see . . . the local pizza shop—"

"After school, sophomore and junior years."

"Lawn mowing."

"Started when I was nine," he tossed back.

"Baby-sitting."

"Only for my sisters, never made a dime."

They were laughing now as Bay racked her brain. "Paper route?"

"Took over my brother's. That was after lawns and before pizza slinging, I think."

"All for medicine?"

"Yes. Goal oriented, remember?"

How could she forget, thought Bay Chandler who had never done more than baby-sit and work summers at the loft because her father had insisted. She couldn't have cared less about school, and it showed. She graduated from Miss Hall's in the lower quarter of her class and put in two years at a fashionable junior college to satisfy the family. Breck had been an escape into the fast lane.

She realized as they headed for the mooring that Paul hadn't asked a thing about her education. Because he already knows all about it, she thought. He already knows....

The tack home was before the wind, and with the sail on a wide beam reach Paul relaxed, putting his arm around her.

"I don't think we have a thing in common except boats," she said in a subdued voice.

His arm tightened around her. "It's a good place to start, Blueblood." His voice was quieter now, too.

At the Chandler mooring, Bay steered while Paul yanked the float out of the water and ran the line through the chock to secure it. They were busy for the next twenty minutes while sails and lines were made shipshape.

By the time the couple returned to the compound, it was dark, and by the time they had finished a cup of coffee on the sofa, it was nearly ten. Paul, visibly tired, had his eyes closed, his head back against the cushions.

"Hard day with the diaper set?"

His lashes swept up, and he found her looking at him. "Mmm. Even tougher than keeping up with a yacht captain who lolls around waiting for the phone to ring."

It hurt. She knew it was meant to make her laugh, but she didn't, couldn't, just now. What *had* she done? She had shopped, made them supper, fed them supper and let herself be sailed across the basin. Big deal.

She looked into her empty mug, feeling his eyes on her, knowing Paul Bendette no longer needed a stethoscope to reach the recesses of her heart.

"How did you do in the Midsummer Series last year?" she asked, reaching for a safe topic.

His arm went around her shoulder. "I was in the top third until I dropped out."

"Dropped out? Quitting doesn't sound like you."

There was a half smile. "Halfway through the summer, I was offered Sunday ER duty—the emergency room at Plymouth General."

"Ah," she said, "a sacrifice for duty." How noble. He was always so damned noble.

"No, the sacrifice was for money. My youngest sister—the last of us—had a chance to go to France with a choral group before she started college. She's at the Boston Conservatory. You'll have to hear her sing sometime, Bay."

"And you paid for the trip. Oh, Paul, that was wonderful." It was wonderful and she felt rotten. It was still a sacrifice for duty, honor, family. She stared harder at her coffee grounds, feeling his fingers move into her hair.

"You're awfully quiet, Blueblood."

She put on a smile. "I'm tired, too."

"How about another shampoo before I take off?"

"You don't have to."

His lips moved to her mouth, kissing her lingeringly before he added, "This is not a sacrifice for duty."

"No," she said getting up, "shampooing probably isn't in the Hippocratic oath."

He followed her the few steps to the bathroom. "Hippocrates didn't know what he was missing."

She let Paul run the taps, busying herself with getting out the shampoo and hair dryer as if it were the most natural, impersonal thing in the world to be bathed by six feet of blond gorgeousness.

Later there would be another fresh bandage and clean curls and her warm, too big, too empty bed, and she would be left to her too big, too empty life, while Paul Bendette went on saving his corner of the world.

The depressing stream of consciousness changed her features. She was staring at the tile above the tub when Paul gently pulled the dryer from her good hand.

"Planning to get in in your shorts and boat shoes, sailor?"

She blinked. "No, as long as you can restrain yourself."

"Do you want me to, Bay? Still?"

Her hazel eyes widened. "Yes," she said out loud. "Things are complicated enough." She worked her feet out of the shoes and her hips out of the shorts.

Paul pulled the rugby shirt over her head and discreetly left her to turn off the water. She was still in her underwear when he turned around, trembling now, even in the June heat. She closed her eyes, afraid he would touch her yet aching for him to touch her.

She gave a tiny gasp when he did. "Bay?"

She bolted for the bedroom, sinking onto the edge of the mattress, not looking up until he told her to. Paul stood in the doorway, his hands in his pockets.

"Look at me. What things are complicated enough?"

"Everything."

He sat down next to her, pulling her good, icy hand into his. "Take the silver spoon out of your mouth and talk to me."

"That's it, you know, the silver spoon. I can't compete, Paul, I can't keep up with your . . . nobility. I feel like I have nothing to offer."

"Nothing to offer! Compete with what? Working my buns off to make ends meet makes me noble?"

"Yes. I know you see me as aimless and spoiled."

He was cupping her chin, now, staring, melting her bones again. "That is the way you see yourself. I see indulged, certainly, but there's been a lot of hurt you never expected, and God knows, you weren't raised to cope with it. That's where I've got the advantage. I'm a whole lot tougher because I've had to be."

Her open hazel eyes had not left his. "And you think you can toughen me up?"

He laughed. "I don't know that I want you tougher, but if you'd start to handle your life the way you handle a boat, you might surprise yourself. You haven't failed just because there have been disappointments."

Paul hugged her as she sat stiffly. "You are self-centered, Whitney Bay, because you think it's safe. You're pulling away right now from me, from facing the things that have crushed you. You're terrified I'm going to mention the miscarriage, too."

She buried her face in his shoulder. "Paul, please, that's enough." She menat it, and she wanted to keep retreating, but the comfort and desire rose so effortlessly in her that she didn't move.

"We'll save it, love. It can wait, and so can the shampoo and the bath. Right now, I'd like to finish what we started last Saturday night."

She raised her face. "I don't suppose you mean dancing?"

No, Jean-Paul Bendette, M.D., did not mean dancing. He meant racing the moon and kissing her senseless, caressing and molding her pliant, aching body to his. When the only scrap of fabric on either of them was the slip of gauze, she paused long enough to pull back the spread and sheet. It gave her an excuse to look at him.

Being seduced by a perfect, blond fantasy had her blood boiling, and for a long time she did very little thinking and lots of feeling. She gasped as he played erotic games over her tense body, finger-walking, massaging, urging her to do the same.

"It's times like this," she moaned, "that I wish I were built like the women in romance novels...that I had what they always do. Paul!" she gasped as he worked his way from the hollow of her throat in a tortuous triangle from one breast to the other.

"You do. A perfect man loves you passionately and is about to prove it."

From beneath him she ran her good hand and the injured one across his back, down his spine to his tight hips. "I meant voluptuous mounds of flesh, the kind men are always cupping in the moonlight as they spiral into ecstasy."

His laugh increased her desire as much as the friction of his rough skin along every inch of her.

His thumb and forefinger began to work the points of her aroused nipples as if he were polishing them. "If you had voluptuous mounds of breasts up here—" his hand slid to the curve of her hip "—then you'd have wide, voluptuous flesh down here."

"Paul."

"Pay attention." His voice came from his throat in a coarse whisper. "Heaven knows, I am." He sucked in a deep breath. "I was about to say that if you had all that, you'd probably be just as irresistible, but you'd be someone else."

"I think you'd like me to be someone else."

His face brushed along hers, and his eyes caught her gaze. "Never—just all that *you* can be. You, darling, are what spirals me into ecstasy."

His eyes closed and then hers did, and it was beyond either of them to do more than savor the intensity and pleasure of the moment. She welcomed him, shutting out all but the sensation of what they meant to each other. It was love at its most exquisite.

Six

When they lay spent and exhausted, Bay ran her fingers over his jaw. "I suppose you think this means I like the idea of your crewing for me every Sunday."

He tickled her ribs. "A minute ago there was no captain, no crew, just equal partners in desire. That's what I like."

"Partners?"

He sat up. "That, too, mostly desire, though."

Paul got her back into the bathroom, and added hot water to the tub. In the midst of the sudsing, he brought up the subject that tore at her. She talked haltingly, facing the tiled walls.

"It's emptiness," she said quietly, "and failure. There were months of 'if only, if only,' until I thought if I didn't get off of St. Thomas, I'd lose my mind."

"Not a whole lot of support from Breck?" The only indication that Paul's probing might have been harder for him than Bay had imagined was the stiffness with which he began to massage her scalp.

She sighed, lifting her head up as he rinsed away the shampoo.

"It wasn't a planned pregnancy as it was. Children don't fit too well into that life-style." She laughed bitterly.

"As a matter of fact, there isn't a lot of room for wives. Breck thought he was supportive, I guess, but deep down the loss was more of a relief. One less responsibility. I came home, saw Dr. Cohen and stayed with Jemmy and Nancy for a few weeks...."

She looked at Paul for the first time in long minutes, finding, just as she knew she would, the concern and compassion of the man who loved her. It gave her the strength to continue.

"By then Breck and I were nearly strangers. None of this did much to enhance my brothers' opinions of my husband, but I don't blame Breck. We had agreed not to start a family. I was trying to be what he wanted and trying to be what my family wanted." She got out of the tub and into the oversize terry robe she had worn for Paul before.

He looked at Breck's monogram. "And still you didn't come home to stay."

"Oh, no. I had sold my parents such a bill of goods about being the world's best captain that I stayed out of sheer stubbornness. Breck kept our Morgan, and I hired on as free-lance, running a Hinkley owned by a couple in New York. I was their investment."

She sat now at the vanity stool. Paul fluffed her wet hair. "But Jeremy knows his little sister like a book and insisted you get your petite buns back to the Cove, or else."

She smiled into the mirror's reflection. "Something like that." While the dryer ran, they were silent, and she watched him, shirtless, dressed only in the jeans he had sailed in. This man loved her.

They finished in the bathroom after eleven. Paul yawned, pointing the way back to bed. She got in after pulling on a lavender T-shirt bearing the logo of a huge smiley-face. Paul sat next to her, changing the dressing.

"Bay, have you ever considered helping other women who go through the trauma of miscarrying?"

There was a lurch in her diaphragm, and unconsciously she moved her hand.

"Whoa," he said gently, tapping her fingertips. "I mean through the hospital or obstetricians' referrals, a support group kind of thing."

"No. I can barely talk about it. How much good would I be for anyone else!"

He looked from the bandage now in place to her guarded expression. "You might be of enormous help to someone else—might help yourself, too. Think about it, darling. Please."

She didn't want to think about it. She wanted Paul to come to bed and pull any thinking right out of her head. She turned away from his blue eyes.

"More than two years is too long not to resolve this."

It was his professional voice, and she spun her head back to look at him. "What would you know about it? You're a man; you haven't even loved someone enough to marry. You've never made a mistake in your whole perfect life!"

His lips pursed. "I'll take that as a compliment."

"It wasn't meant as one." She watched him pick up his shirt, put it on and tuck it into his jeans. "What are you doing?"

He sat down again and turned his face toward her. "Put those arms around my neck."

"Why?" She didn't move.

"Because it feels so good."

She did, reluctantly. It felt wonderful. He was whispering and that felt stimulating until she started to listen. "I'm going home," he said.

"What?" She pulled away, genuinely surprised and hurt.

"I'm the pediatrician for a tiny village. The goldfish bowl nearly did you in Wednesday night. I love you, Bay, every tight little inch, but I am protecting you, as well as myself. I live over the office—"

"Propriety," she said sourly.

"This isn't the islands."

"No, it certainly isn't. It's all right to make love, of course, just as long as nobody finds out."

"Bay, please. You've been in town less than a week. I'm thinking of you, too."

She looked from Paul to the sliding doors and the deck outside. "It's happening too fast, isn't it?"

He brought her face around to his. "For you, maybe. You're trusting and terrified of what you feel because you work so bloody hard at not feeling anything."

She looked back, knowing he was talking about far more than just their relationship. "I've waited a long time for this, for you," he said.

"I'll let you down," she whispered.

"I doubt it."

"I'm spoiled and self-centered and—"

"Scared to death," he added.

He was getting too close. She closed her eyes. "I was going to say, 'and great in bed.'"

Paul laughed out loud, hugging her till her ribs hurt, kissing her with longing more intense than it had been moments earlier. He moaned, "Chivalry is hell," and slid off the mattress. "I have office hours till noon. I'll call."

At the sliding doors he turned back. "Think about my suggestion, a support group."

She nodded reluctantly and waved him off with her wrapped hand. She was already aching from his absence.

It was noon by the time Paul called, and the call was an apology. "Tied up all morning," he said into the phone with a yawn, "but I'm free soon. Weather doesn't look too promising, but we could sail if you'd like."

Bay looked out at the shifting clouds. "I'd like. Rain's predicted for tomorrow, you know."

"I heard. There's a chance we won't get to boss each other around."

Bay sighed. "Not on the boat, anyway."

"You're tired," she said to him when he finally climbed to the deck at two. His face was drawn with fatigue.

He kissed her. "You kept me up too late. You and the two calls I got after I checked my service."

"I hope it wasn't anything too serious," she said, feeling, however, as though he took it to mean that she still didn't want to face her own problems.

"Nothing that's kept me from you."

They did sail that afternoon, although Bay was allowed to do little more than to shift her weight. The unfavorable breeze was strong, and they joined hundreds of other weekend sailors offshore, many of whom were fellow Scots also out for a trial run. With Bay at the tiller they even flew the spinnaker for the downwind leg, settling next to each other for the long reach home.

They were in yellow foul-weather slickers, salty from the spray. As they furled the sails at the mooring, Paul kissed her. "This is one of the ways I like you best," he said.

"Care to name the others?"

"Soon," he replied, "very soon."

Or so he said. Once he drove back to the compound, Bay insisted on fixing dinner. Paul nodded over another yawn, pulling off the weatherproof jacket and plopping himself on her couch. She tugged gently on his wrist. "How about a nap while I make dinner?"

He smiled sleepily. "Maybe a little one." He got up and draped his arms around her.

Bay laughed, moving him in the direction of her bed. "Lie down. You're dead on your feet. Let me fool around in the kitchen for a while, and you can fool around with me later. Save the bedside manner for dessert."

He agreed, and with him stretched out on her bed, she set to work, bandage and all, concocting a simple dinner. When the rice was set to boil, she fixed herself a cranberry fizz and checked on her guest. It was dusk now, after six and cloudy. Paul had pulled off the spread and lay on his side, his eyes closed, his features slack as though he had fallen asleep effortlessly. His even breathing was the only sound in the room as Bay watched for a moment, biting her lips at the waves of affection welling up in her.

Affection. It wasn't even desire at the moment, just deep contentment. The pitching and shifting inside her was subsiding, thanks to the man asleep on her pillow. She smiled at her thoughts. This man thinks he loves me. She watched the rise and fall of his chest, trying out the idea of being lovable after all. He was a bolt out of the Newport night. She shook her head and left him to his dreams.

At seven when dinner was ready, she tiptoed back into the bedroom and put a hand on his shoulder. "Hey, sailor," she whispered, "dinnertime."

There was no response; she tried again. "Paul, chowtime!"

He stirred, rolled onto his back, bending an elbow over his eyes against the bedside lamp she flicked on. "You eat, love. I'll get up in a little while."

"Chicken tarragon." Sort of chicken tarragon. She had put on two breasts of chicken and sprinkled the herb on it. It smelled pretty good, actually.

"Great. Five more minutes." She could tell he was falling into heavy sleep again, and she felt a bolt of fear. Perhaps he had been up all night with some terrible emergency and hadn't told her.

Not quite as euphoric as she had been, Bay returned to the kitchen, raised the lid on the frying pan and jabbed the chicken with her serving fork.

"Chicken for one." She ate it with the rice and salad, toasting her sleeping dinner companion with her cranberry juice and chiding herself for the irritation she felt. Exhaustion was probably a fact of Paul's life. There would probably be constant dinners alone. She realized she was putting things in the future tense and abruptly finished her plate of food.

By nine o'clock the man had had enough of a nap, Bay decided. Desperate times called for desperate measures. When she flicked on the light beside him again, she was naked. "Dr. Bendette!"

His eyes flew open, focused and closed. "I must be dreaming!"

"Remember me, sailor?" She sat down on the edge of the bed.

His eyes were still closed, and his fingers walked over her ribs. "The face is familiar. Newport, I think. Moonlight and hysteria. It's all coming back." His thumb and index finger massaged one soft nipple and the creamy skin around it until she moaned.

"I seem to recall mounds of cleavage that night, however. Voluptuousness. Let me think, Sheila Dunlap?"

"Wrong!" Laughing, Bay straddled him, digging her good hand into his hair.

His hands steadied her hips as he looked up at her. "Not Sheila? Let me try again. There's something familiar about this spot, too, and this and these, just the way they are." He cupped both her breasts and raised himself up to kiss them and her. "Didn't you faint in my arms?"

She played with his belt buckle, staring back with her own gleam. "Who's Sheila Dunlap?" The buckle separated in her fingers, and the zipper teeth of his pants parted.

Paul's voice was noticeably tighter. "Someone I knew once. You're not the only one with a tragic romance." There didn't seem to be any tragedy in his voice, however, only passion and sleep. "My God, woman, is this the way you wake all your dinner guests?"

She gave him her most devilish grin. "Only my crew. How's your appetite?"

Strong masculine hands grabbed her shoulders, pulling her down. "Ravenous. Can't you tell?"

"Yes," she gasped, thinking only briefly of the cold chicken in the iron skillet. "It's a good thing, too. The appetizer's now being served."

When Paul got around to the main course, Bay sat watching him. She sipped another cranberry juice. "Sheila Dunlap."

"Ring a bell?" he asked.

"Should it?"

He shook his head. "No."

She put her hand over his free one. "Tragic?"

"At the time. But we were young. Way too young. I had miles to go, as they say. I wasn't what she wanted."

"No kidding. I can't imagine you not being what every woman wants."

He grinned. "Thanks. I like your train of thought."

With the possible exception of her older brother, there wasn't another person alive who could read her moods the way this man could. It overwhelmed her to think that she was so transparent, so easily understood, when she tried so hard to mask her emotions.

She picked up his plate as he pushed himself from the table. "You make it hard to be mysterious, Doc."

"Leave that to Greta Garbo. Bare your soul to me, trust me with it."

Like I just did with my body, she thought.

He was behind her at the sink, taking the dishes from her hands and nuzzling her ear. "You'll never regret it."

Thunder rolled in the distance as she turned to him and encircled his waist with her arms. "You expect so much. You make everything look so effortless, so easy. Falling in love . . . saving lives, juggling profession and personal life—''

''I haven't figured out how to manage sleep too well.''

She laughed and let him go. ''Do you always fall in love this easily?''

''Always?''

''Never mind,'' she said, not wanting any more details than she already had.

Bay slept alone, regretting Paul's departure more intensely the second time than the first. The storm had rolled in, hitting the Cove with driving rain. From her bed she could see the flashes of lightning lighting the water. She was awake half the night, talking herself out of being frightened, longing, for the first time, for the return of her family. She was not a loner. She thrived on company, on family, on children. It took a long time to fall asleep.

Bay awoke at seven-thirty to the steady patter. The rain had slackened but showed no signs of letting up. The race would certainly be called off. It was less certain that she could still make something of the day.

After breakfast she phoned Paul only to be told by his service that he had been called to the hospital. And if the weather had cleared, she thought, I would have had to forfeit the race.

He called back at ten. ''Brunch,'' he said, ''or shall we just make love all day?''

''Don't you ever identify yourself?''

''Good Lord, woman, how much identification do you need?''

She laughed, biting back the urge to ask if he would have given up the race, had there been one. ''How do you know I didn't scoot back to Newport after you left last night?''

"Because I'm all you can handle. Across a crowded room you thought I was fantastic, and up close I'm even better.''

She savored her body's response to his teasing then cleared her throat. "It's your humility that's so irresistible. Humble, just like your background. But I think you're turning *me* into a fantasy.''

"You may be right,'' he said. "My fantasy for the moment is taking a rich girl to lunch.''

"And you're buying?'' she asked.

"Yup.''

"Gee, I'd meet you somewhere, but driving Jeremy's stick shift is against my doctor's orders.'' She didn't mention the shopping trip or her other minor excursions.

"I like a woman who takes orders.''

"Good,'' she threw back, finishing the conversation. "Let me know when you find one.''

An hour later she was sitting, dressed for Sunday brunch, at a laminated plastic table with a tray before her, munching a muffin and sipping very bad coffee.

"Just for future reference, Doc, rich girls do not think hospital cafeterias qualify as elegant luncheon fare.''

Paul grinned. "I don't remember a thing about *elegant*.''

"No,'' she said, "you probably don't. As a rich person, I just assumed you'd whisk me up to Boston. The Ritz would have been nice, even Zachary's.'' She raised her eyes and added the part she'd held back purposely. "Paul, you've already explained about the late-night call over here, but there's more to it than just wanting to be with me, isn't there?''

"Perceptive little sailor."

"We're not sailing—"

"No, we're not. You're right. I'm giving you the opportunity to talk to a woman named Audrey Parker. She had a miscarriage on Friday. She'll be leaving tomorrow with empty arms, as they say. Just like you did."

Bay opened her mouth to protest, only to be silenced by Paul's fingers on her lips. "What she needs is someone to listen. She and her husband are from Michigan; there's no extended family here to help. She'll be fine, but the chance to have someone to support her will make her recovery—"

"Everything mine was not."

He looked surprised. "I thought you might use some empathy."

"By opening my own wound?"

"It never healed! You have as much to gain as she does, but I won't push. She's here, seventh floor. Unfortunately she's still on the maternity wing, not the gynecology. I've told her about you." He looked at his watch. "She was far more receptive to the idea than you, by the way."

Paul took their trays and got up. "I'll be finished in about an hour. You can wait for me in the doctors' lounge after you've finished. Take as much time as you need. I'll sleep there while I wait, if I get the chance."

Bay pushed her hand against the flush she knew was coloring her face. He was asking the impossible.

"What if I fall apart?"

YOURS ABSOLUTELY FREE.

Did you know that Silhouette Romances are not available from the shops in the U.K?

Read on to discover how you could receive four brand new Silhouette Romances FREE and without obligation, as your introductory offer to Silhouette Reader Service.

As thousands of women who have read these books know — Silhouette Romances sweep you away into an exciting love filled world of fascination between men and women. A world filled with age old conflicts — love and money, ambition and guilt, jealousy and pride. Silhouette Romances are the latest stories written by the world's best romance writers and they are only available from Reader Service. As a regular reader you could enjoy 6 brand new titles every month delivered direct to your door, post and packing free, plus an exclusive Newsletter bringing you all the latest information on the top Silhouette authors as well as recipes, competitions, and extra bargain offers.

And by way of introduction we will send you four specially selected Silhouette Romance novels plus an exclusive Silhouette TOTE BAG FREE when you complete and return this card.

FREE TOTE BAG as your introduction to **Silhouette Romances**

"Grief is part of healing. Audrey needs to fall apart, too. Love, I'm due back on Pediatrics. The doctors' lounge is just through those doors to the right. Okay?"

"You won't be angry if I refuse?" You'll just be disappointed and I'll never hear from you again, she added silently to herself. There was a real stab of fear in her.

His voice was low. "Anger has nothing to do with this, you know that." He kissed her lightly and moved from the stainless-steel countertops where they had left the trays.

"Paul?" It was barely above a whisper. "Will you ride the elevator with me?"

Brunch or not, her stomach felt hollow, her heart heavy and her hands sweaty. Hospitals all smell the same, she thought as she watched Paul tap the seventh-floor button on the elevator. Medicinal, disinfected, impersonal. The long ride up six flights reminded her how she hated them, and how she had suffered without anyone at her side but Breck in Charlotte Amalie.

What color she had had in her face in the cafeteria drained away as the steel doors opened. "I need a doctor," she whispered.

Paul grinned. "You've got one."

Ignoring the paging of staff and the new mothers and husbands who were shuffling in the corridors, she leaned against Paul, trying to concentrate on holding down her anxiety.

The bustle was distracting. "I started you out during visiting hours," he said, skirting a group. "If this works out—"

"It won't."

He ignored her. "I'll arrange for clearance, and you can work out a schedule convenient with the patient."

She was angry. "You've already got me running a support group! Paul, I have no qualifications. I have no skills for this."

"You have them all."

"You're out of your mind."

He kissed her again. "Ain't love grand. This is it. Have me paged if you need to. I love you, Bay."

"I know. That's what got me into this mess."

Audrey Parker was sitting up in bed in a semiprivate room. Her half of the room was smothered in flowers. It masked the medicinal smell, but the perfume of blooming hothouse arrangements was just as cloying. Audrey was young, in her mid-twenties at most, her makeup fresh, her hair clean. But when she turned to Bay, there was a dead light in her brown eyes—nothing more than a curiously flat gaze.

Bay extended her hand, bandaged though it was, which Audrey shook lightly, and then Bay pulled up a chair.

"Dr. Bendette said you might stop in." She looked at her hands and then at the sheet. "He would have been the baby's pediatrician."

Bay was already searching for some words of comfort. Her tongue felt swollen and useless, and the anxiety she had dreaded washed over her. "I know," she said.

Audrey began to talk. "I was barely through the first trimester. There was no chance of survival, of course. Hardly even a little person. We can try again. I'm only twenty-four." The broken sentences tumbled out as she avoided Bay's eyes. "I'm okay, really."

Bay touched her arm. "You sound as though you're quoting what everyone else has had to say to cheer you up. You don't have to be brave for me, Audrey. I thought maybe if I came and listened—'' She didn't know where to go from there. Her face, so neatly made-up, began to crumple. Another bolt of fear went through Bay.

"Thank goodness," Audrey choked.

"You have every right to grieve, no matter how early in the pregnancy it was. It's not your fault."

As if she were waiting for permission or compassion or simply the presence of another woman, the young patient sighed, her eyes welling with tears. Bay held her hand, the moment transporting her back to her own bed, her own desolation. Together they wept.

Seven

Bay stayed with Audrey longer than she had ever intended, long enough to see that she was doing some good. It was obvious from the patient's change of attitude that Bay was a real help. The episode left her churning inside, and after they exchanged phone numbers, she left for the doctors' lounge.

Paul was asleep, as he had said he would be. Her first instinct was to leave him, but she was becoming increasingly agitated by the hospital environment. Just anxiety, she kept reminding herself as she waited for him on the fake leather couch in the hall.

They were halfway home when Paul mentioned that he was proud of her. "You made a real difference, I'm sure."

"That remains to be seen. You can turn off the windshield wipers. The rain has stopped."

His hand went to the knob, his eyes still trained on the slick road. "Are you going to change the subject every time this is mentioned?"

"It isn't raining." Her voice was close to a whine, and Paul glanced over at her, but he didn't add a thing until she flicked on the radio. He turned it off.

"I'm going to drop you off at the boathouse and get back to the hospital." Fine muscles tensed along his jaw.

"Paul! Is this punishment because I don't want to talk about my miscarriage?"

"Oh, for God's sake, Bay, of course not! I have a sixteen-year-old coming out of surgery, who wrapped himself around a tree last night."

"And if the weather had been perfect, we would have had to forfeit the race today, wouldn't we?"

He looked over to her again. "The weather wasn't perfect."

"But if it had been?"

His car lurched along the Chandler grounds until he killed the engine at the boathouse. "Sick children have terrible timing," he added.

"I wouldn't know."

"That's enough, Bay. I love you, I understand your grief and I'm trying my damnedest to help you face it, but if you're going to throw garbage like forfeiting a race at me every time my career gets in the way, we're in big trouble."

"Your career didn't get in the way. You dragged me over there to dredge up memories."

"So you can get on with your life. So we can get on with some sort of relationship." The boathouse was shrouded in a fine mist. Bay got out into the seemingly liquid air that surrounded her and then Paul.

"It seems to me, Paul, that a relationship is based on something far deeper than what we have."

"And what is that?" He stood in front of her, his hands shoved into his pants pockets. She could hear the jingle of his car keys.

"A week's worth of flirting, mostly. A night of crazy behavior followed by a lot of heavy breathing, as far as I can tell," was her answer.

He watched her. "That's how you see this?"

She nodded.

"I don't know," he said, shrugging. "I kind of like the heavy breathing."

"Be serious."

He reached for her, holding her at arm's length. "What's the point in that? Every time I attempt to be serious, you back away like a child at a fire. You want to play it for laughs, Bay? If you want to treat this no more seriously than the rest of your life, I'm not your man. I know that much about myself. I'm ready. I've worked my tail off for my future, for the children of this town, for my own satisfaction."

One of his hands left her arm and raked through his damp hair. She shivered. "I want more from this summer with you than sex and a twenty-one-foot sailboat, Bay."

"Maybe that's all I'm capable of giving."

"You're working damn hard at making me believe it."

Abruptly she turned from him and started the climb to her apartment. Her back tingled with the expectation of his arms stopping her. There was nothing.

At the top of the gray banister she paused and looked down at his back as he opened the car door. Go back and save the world, Dr. Bendette, just don't expect me to be able to help. The door shut; the engine hummed. Not another word passed between them.

When the phone rang at five, she leaped for it, her hand on her heart. It had to be Paul.

"Hey, Kiddo! How's the solitary life?" Jeremy sounded cheerful.

"Wonderful," she lied, trying not to sound too disappointed.

"Did you race today?"

"Rained out." And don't ask who I got for crew, she implored silently.

"Who did you get for crew?"

"Nobody you know. How did *you* do?"

"Top ten. Are you changing the subject?"

Bay laughed. "Of course not. Paul Bendette is crewing for me. I met him by accident, thereby saving you a dinner invitation. He was at Sea Mist, as it turns out." There! She had given him enough truth that the omissions would never be noticed.

"What do you think of him?"

"Knows his stuff, which is not surprising, Newport and all."

In the pause that followed, older brother waited for younger sister to offer more provocative information. Bay knew Jeremy every bit as well as Jeremy knew Bay. All he got was the crackle of the open line between Alden's Cove, Massachusetts, and Hamilton, Bermuda.

"Just think," he said finally, "you could have knocked him off his feet in Newport instead of seducing the security guard."

"I didn't *seduce* anybody. Paul's not my type, anyway," she lied.

Jeremy changed the subject back to the Chandlers, events on the island, chitchat about their own celebrating and their return to the compound.

She talked to her mother and Christopher's wife and then hung up, thinking now about her one enchanted evening.

There was no stranger across a crowded room that night or the next. Bay had no dinner partners, no offers for a shampoo. The morning of the Fourth of July, she received a call from Paul's answering service telling her that he had been caught in Boston after he had transferred a patient to the Children's Hospital. She thought immediately of the teenager who had been in the accident and felt guiltier than ever.

Audrey Parker called, which further reminded her of the turmoil created by Jean-Paul Bendette, M.D. Nevertheless she accepted a last-minute invitation to celebrate with Audrey and her husband.

There was a plea in Audrey's voice, one that became less evident when Bay arrived. They spent the day watching the village's old-fashioned parade, going to a concert given by the high-school dance band and picnicking on the beach under the clearing weather. The heat was returning. Paul, of course, came up in the day's conversations. Audrey, it appeared, thought he deserved sainthood. Her spirits were steadily improving, and she gave credit to Paul and Bay.

"Just getting off the maternity floor was a big help, but what I really needed was you, someone to listen." Her eyes glistened. "I'm working through this one day at a time." Her smile was brave.

The miscarriage was a ribbon woven through the day but neither the focus nor the purpose of the visit. Their conversation touched on sailing, the Cove and on life in general. It cheered Bay as much as it cheered Audrey, and at the end of the day when they stood at the Triumph, Audrey gave her a hug.

"I feel as though I've made a friend through all this."

Bay hugged her back. "So do I, and I think I needed this as much as you did."

Audrey stepped away, her arm now around her husband's waist. "I hope you won't stop with me. This area needs a support group, and you'd be perfect for starting one. I know it would help me get through these first weeks when you think everything is your fault."

Bay left, promising to be in touch, buoyed by the realization that she had made a difference. Paul was right and she knew it.

The next morning at nine was her appointment to have the sutures removed. She'd be a new woman! Someone who could go back to washing her own hair. She didn't want to go back to washing her own hair, however. She planned to tell Paul that as he removed the tiny row of black threads.

She had half a mind to show up in a T-shirt as outlandish as the one she'd worn that first morning, but opted, instead, for a new green skirt and oversize blouse. Positively *Vogue* magazine—and all for the doctor she hadn't seen since Sunday.

She wondered how his week had been, about his fatigue, his successes and his failures. She wondered if he had missed her. Men who fell in love so easily might fall out of love just as quickly. Her palms were moist again.

Fifteen minutes before her appointment, she drove the sports car out along Pilgrim's Point to the office. With her stomach in knots, she entered the office. The contrast to her visit the week before was as dramatic as her own change of clothes.

The toys, which had been so neatly stacked the last time she'd seen them, lay scattered. Two toddlers battled over a Fisher-Price truck, and another was methodically tearing pages from a worn issue of *Ladies' Home Journal*. Mothers attempted to soothe their infants, and from behind the door of the first examining room where she knew Mickey and Donald floated from the ceiling, came a piercing wail.

Bay gave the receptionist her name, marveling at the fact that the woman could field phone calls, take payments from women with straddling infants on their hips and ignore the chaos. It was business as usual, and there was not a male in sight.

It struck Bay that it was amazing the pediatrician was able to put a sentence together after a whole day of coping with this. After Bay had waited for five minutes on the couch, the nurse-practitioner came through another door and motioned for the toddler hugging the truck to follow her. He did, with his mother and sister in tow. A moment later the wailing infant and her mother appeared at the door of the examining room. Bay caught a glimpse of Mickey and Pluto on their strings, and heard the mother thanking Dr. Bendette profusely. "Thanks so much for squeezing us in," she said, her hand extended.

The sound of Paul's reply turned Bay's insides to bubbling glue. For the next ten minutes Bay sat staring at a *National Geographic*, reminding herself that Paul hadn't called because he had been too busy. He'd been out of town, and he'd probably been irritated with her behavior. She looked at a full-page color photograph of an iguana. I can be very irritating, she told herself, and now I am a total basket case.

When she looked up from the article about the Galápagos Islands, Paul—stethoscope around his neck, short-sleeved oxford shirt, gorgeous forearms and all—was leaning over the shoulder of his receptionist. It wouldn't have surprised her to see a white horse in the parking lot.

Without even seeing Bay, he scooped a small boy up into his arms and went back into the examining room, followed by a teary mother.

The nurse-practitioner called her name and motioned Bay to follow her into the adjoining room. She jumped to her feet, the magazine sliding off her lap.

It was not until she was sitting on the examining table, listening to the idle chitchat of Paul's associate that Bay realized the sutures were about to be removed by the woman. Paul Bendette obviously had far more urgent ills to attend to.

Ten minutes later, having given the receptionist her medical insurance number, Bay picked up the *National Geographic* and left the office. The butterflies that had been sailing around in her stomach were now deadweight under her ribs. Across the crowded room they hadn't even made eye contact. She got into the Triumph. He was acting as though he knew what was best for her. That was the hell of it. He did. He was what she needed.

The thin red scar was pain free, so Bay concentrated on planning her day with Audrey Parker. She took a long hot shower then cooled the water and washed her hair, working up a good healthy lather. She tried to work up a good healthy distaste for men who knew what was best for her and then left her alone to find out for herself. She wasn't terribly successful.

She ate an early supper and called the Parkers. There was enough tide and daylight for an impromptu sail, and the three of them cruised the harbor in the Flying Scot with Bay at the helm. Not once did anyone grab the tiller or help her yank the sheet. In fact, the Parkers complimented her profusely, joked about following her back to St. Thomas for a real cruise and made her promise to ask them to go sailing again.

When they parted at their cars, Ned Parker put his arm around his wife. "This is the best she's been all week. We have you to thank."

Bay shook her head. "You two have each other and that helps." When she was finally alone, Bay sank her head onto Jeremy's steering wheel and repeated her parting words. They hurt.

She had to scrub the cuff of her sleeve over her eyes to clear her vision. She slowed the Triumph at the lane to the compound, and while she waited for two cars to pass, she decided to take fate into her own hands. She swatted off the blinker, shifted the car through its gears and headed out to Pilgrim's Point.

The headlights of the low-slung car bathed the driveway, bouncing from the shrubbery to the front of the office. A single car sat in the lot, and the light from the waiting room filled the office window. It wasn't Paul's car.

Nevertheless, Bay got out, trotted up to the door and pulled open the screen. The waiting room was quiet and as neat as when she had first seen it. The receptionist sat at her desk, immersed in paperwork. She looked up in surprise.

"Dr. Bendette has gone for the night. Have you called his service?"

Bay shook her head. "This is a personal call. I just thought I might find him in."

The woman smiled. "He could use some personal calls, if you ask me. 'Course he doesn't ask me. He's going to wind up like his patients if he doesn't stop driving himself." She looked sympathetic. "You missed him by more than an hour. Lord only knows when he'll be back from Plymouth General. Shall I tell him you were here?"

Bay shook her head, hoping she didn't look as disappointed and foolish as she felt. She didn't leave, however. She stood by her car in the dark, looking up at the dark dormer windows, and then she took the bull by the horns.

She got a pencil and a scrap of paper from her purse and wrote:

Prince Charming,
Cinderella is waiting for a house call. Come and check the suture scar. I'm covered by medical insurance and not much else.

C.

She giggled but her hand trembled, and she knew if she stopped to reread it, she'd lose her nerve. Instead she went to the second door at the front of the house, stuck the note between the screen and the frame and left.

By the time her own place bounced into view in the headlights, she was full of uncertainty. She shouldn't have left it. He would think she was too aggressive; he would think she was wacko. Then again, he already thought she was crazy. A stream of consciousness and "he'll thinks" were still running through her brain as she climbed the stairs and found, tucked into the frame of the sliding doors, a note written on a physician's prescription pad.

She read every word twice, including the letterhead.

The script was surprisingly legible, considering his line of work.

Bay,
I should have guessed you'd hit the Scot the minute your bandage came off. The view from here was great. You're not a bad sailor, considering the missing crew member. Stayed long enough to watch you sail into the sunset.

J.P.

Lord, what that man did to her digestive system. She laughed out loud, full of relief and affection and the desire to be back in his arms. Sleep seemed impossible; nevertheless, she was in bed by eleven. When she began to drift off to sleep finally, she was lulled by the sounds of the sea and the night and her pounding pulse.

She awoke in the dark to the sound of Paul's footsteps on her staircase. From her bed she watched his dark, recognizable shadow come across the balcony to the bedroom sliding doors. The silhouette slid the screen back, turned to close it and stood at the foot of the bed.

"You shouldn't have left that unlocked," he said quietly.

"I've been expecting you," she whispered back, her ears full of the wash of her own pulse.

He undressed, throwing his clothes on the chair. Her toes began to tingle, a sensation that worked its way north as she lay beneath the sheet. She watched his shadow as he walked toward her. One hip undulated and then the other, and then he, clean and warm, slid in next to her. She was about to whisper his name when his mouth brushed her lips.

He tasted of toothpaste, and the sensation of his body sliding over hers drove her hands—both of them now—into his hair. Shampoo, soap, toothpaste... She moaned, feeling the planes of his face, his jaw, his shoulders.

"Remember me?" he said at last.

She was eager for the game. "Let me think," she whispered back, the pads of her fingers patting his collarbone. "I feel indentations here, stethoscope?" Then she moved down his spine, loving the gasp it brought from his chest. "Lovely back, a medicinal smell from hospital corridors..."

Her fingers came around from his hips to his chest. She felt his muscles tighten as she worked her hand between her body and his and then inched lower.

"There ought to be something familiar down here," she said with a groan as he arched and wrapped her in his arms. She laughed a little. "Now this I recognize."

"I was hoping you would," he said, finishing the conversation and the game, leading her from there in the pursuit of pure pleasure until there was nothing in her head but the sensation that she was loved more deeply and strongly than she had ever been in her life.

Eight

For a woman who doesn't want to communicate, you're coming through loud and clear," Paul finally whispered.

Bay sighed into the hollow of his shoulder. "I'm not sure this solves anything."

His warm lips brushed her mouth. "Don't take the joy out of it, Bay. It doesn't have to solve anything. You tried to find me tonight and I tried to find you. That says an awful lot right there. I need you in my life—"

"There's hardly room for me in your life. I don't even get to see you when I have an appointment!"

He was growing serious. "Which is one more reason why you've got to have a life of your own. You are capable of touching people's lives, of making a difference, and I know damn well, sooner or later you'll see that just as I do."

She sat up, hugging her knees. "I think I should straighten out my own life first, don't you? You're pushing me, Paul, always pushing."

He came up in the dark, too, propped on one elbow. "It's about time someone did. You've gotten away with murder for twenty-eight years. Don't misunderstand me; I think your family's great, but it's time you started acting like one of them. There's not another Chandler I know who sits around analyzing what went wrong with life."

"Nothing's gone wrong with any of their lives! Can't you see that? Can't you see my brothers and their careers, their perfect children, their perfect marriages? My mother and her commitments... Chris's wife juggles family and a job...my father still puts in an eight-hour day—" With a sigh she fell back into the pillows, staring into the gray, dim light.

"All my life they've given me everything I ever wanted, let me do whatever I thought was important, and I blew it, completely."

"You sail like the wind, and it's more than an idle pastime for you."

"Thanks, but I can't even slice a grapefruit without botching it."

Paul kissed the palm. "Yes, but look what good came of that."

Bay laughed reluctantly and pulled his head from her hand to her breasts. "You're driving me crazy, Jean-Paul."

"But doesn't it feel good?"

"You want too much from me," she answered.

He brought his face up to hers. "I want the best for you. I want you to stop letting fear motivate you."

"You sound like a doctor."

"I am one. You were afraid to talk with Audrey Parker because of the risk. Didn't that turn out for the best? You're afraid to eat in public places with me for fear of what people are saying. Hell, Bay, you flirted your little heart out when you thought I was just another gorgeous face—"

He stopped and gave her time to react to the quip, but she was quiet. "We make love in your bed, darling, and you still can't admit that you're falling in love because it means giving up yourself, trusting *me* with your feelings."

Her fingers, which had been gripping the sheet, yanked it over her head. From underneath it she said, "Trust has gotten me nowhere. I told you I have lousy taste in men."

"Au contraire."

"God," she groaned from under the sheet, "now he's going to spout off in French."

"I can make love in two languages."

She brought the percale down to her breasts. "There is no end to your talent." She meant it.

He kissed her again. "And no end to yours. Give yourself to those who need you. Women like Audrey need you. I need you. You make a difference in our lives, honestly."

Her chest was aching now from his honesty. She moved to hug him, but he pivoted away from her and snapped on her bedside lamp.

"I knew it!" she cried. "You're leaving again. How can you do this? You yell and scream at me, make love to me, speak French to me, for heaven's sake, then roll over and go home? I must be out of my mind.

"Get out! I don't want you here for an hour of fooling around, Paul. I mean it. Your middle-class morality is too much. You're wrong about the restaurant. I'm old news; you and I are old news."

Her steam was building, stoked by frustration with herself as much as with him. "You want proper then we'll keep it proper. We'll go on dates and you'll drive me home. You'll kiss me good-night at the door. Period! I don't need you. I can't let myself need you, can't you see that? Because the minute I do, you're gone, back to your nice safe bed over the office."

She chewed her lip and drove her hands through her hair, but he pulled her sharply to him, and for a moment she lay pressed against him, feeling both their hearts pound against each other.

"I'm not going home," he said at last. "I went back to my apartment to shower and change because I have to return to the hospital now. It can't be helped." His voice was matter-of-fact, but she could feel his fatigue, the weight of his chest as she held him and was held. They were silent while she thought about how to apologize.

"Forgive me," she murmured, "for *this* time, then." There was more silence; words formed in her head and then fell away until she pulled back and looked into those honest blue eyes.

"Don't leave angry like the last time," she added. "Everything is happening so fast that I'm afraid of what I feel and of how much. It's deeper than I ever dreamed, Paul, and scaring the wits out of me."

"I know," he answered. "It's scaring the wits out of me, too."

"So the man of steel has doubts?"

"Not about us." He got up, reaching for his clothes.

Bay sat in the lamplight, watching him pull on his clothes. "Paul, I want to make a deal."

He turned to her, tucking in his shirt. "Shoot."

"My entire family comes home next week. I want one whole night with you before that. That gives you a few days to figure out how you're going to do it and, as a matter of fact, I don't intend to sit around the boat-house waiting for the decision, either. You pick the night and hope I haven't made other plans. I have friends to see and boats to sail."

He was grinning, buttoning his shirt and shaking his head. "Feisty, even out of bed. You've got yourself a deal."

She saw Audrey Parker again the next day, Friday, and they talked less of their mutual loss and more about the rest of their lives. They had things in common, re-moved from children, and by the end of that day Bay felt she had found a friend.

Bay's first invitation to Paul's apartment was for that evening, an invitation so full of yawns that she insisted on making dinner. Their interlude the previous night had taken the place of a nap, and the good doctor had not slept in twenty-four hours.

She arrived at Pilgrim's Point at six with a cold ham salad, brownies, marinated vegetables and a jug of iced tea. Upon arrival she found that Paul's living quarters comprised the entire second story of the house.

Paul was asleep in the living room on the couch, an open copy of *The New England Journal of Medicine* over his lap. His back windows overlooked the tennis courts of a neighboring house, and the slap of a ball and cheers from a foursome drifted up.

The rooms were stuffy and hot, holding the July heat just under the roof. They needed straightening. On the kitchen counter there was a bottle of wine cooling in an ice bucket and what looked to be a week's worth of un-opened mail. It stirred her, his catch-as-catch-can exis-tence, but the only thing she straightened was a loose lock of his yellow hair. Her fingernail across his fore-head brought his eyes open.

"You found me," he said.

She smiled. "I knew you were under this clutter somewhere."

He sat up, letting the medical journal slide onto the floor. "I was going to clean up for you, but I thought I'd better save my strength. You said you wanted a night together. Wanna curl up here on the sofa with me till morning?"

Bay stood up, laughing. "No way! If I have one night with you, it better not be this one. I'll be lucky to get a meal into you."

Paul stretched, and she could feel him watch her as she walked back to the kitchen alcove. She found plates and wineglasses and motioned him to the little drop-leaf table when everything was ready. He was still stretch-ing.

"Do you always drive yourself this hard?" Bay asked as she served the ham salad.

He nodded. "It's what I do."

"And what if you get called out tonight?"

"I won't. Plymouth Pediatrics is covering for me. Saturday, too. That's when I'm all yours."

Bay arched her eyebrows. "Saturday, all day?"

Paul laughed. "Hard to believe, isn't it?"

"And Sunday for the race?"

"Yup."

She looked at him. "Two whole days. I'm more ir-resistible than I thought."

They talked about tennis, the race, Audrey Parker and the return of the Chandlers, tonsils, rubella and the mediocre wine. Paul was fading noticeably by his second brownie. Bay stood up, dinner plates in hand, as Paul suggested he put on a pot of coffee.

With one sandaled foot, she pointed in the direction of the bedroom. "Hit the bed. I'll do the dishes, tuck you in and leave. No coffee."

It was barely dusk. "The night is young, Cinderella...."

"The doctor is exhausted, Prince Charming. You're so good at tossing around orders, let's see you follow a few. Just like I'll do Sunday at the helm," she added, turning her back and marching into the kitchen.

In the few minutes it took to scrape the dishes and put them in his dishwasher, the apartment grew quiet. When she had finished, she tiptoed into the bedroom. It was just big enough for a double bed, dresser, mirror and bookshelf. Like the living room, it was crammed with texts, dog-eared paperbacks and discarded clothes. A handful of family snapshots sat on the dresser; a few were stuck in the mirror, including one of a blonde with an outdated hairstyle.

Paul was awake. "Sheila?" Bay asked, sitting on the edge of the bed.

"That really bothers you, doesn't it?" he said.

"A woman likes to know her competition."

His blue eyes coursed over her face. "She's no longer competition. It's an old picture I keep around for no reason. You met your competition downstairs. There's hundreds of them for that matter."

"All clamoring for a piece of you."

Paul closed his eyes, and she kissed them. "I know, it's what you do." She had been running her hand lightly over his bare shoulder in an absentminded gesture of affection, stopping as she heard him sigh.

"Don't stop," he said, but she pushed his head back into the depths of his pillow and stood up, lifting the sheet as she did. She looked down toward his knees.

"Insatiable," he muttered. "I admire that in a woman."

"You certainly got out of your clothes in a hurry. Save your strength. It's seven o'clock. If you sleep now, you'll get a good ten or twelve hours."

Paul rolled onto his side. "Unless some hysterical brunette cuts her hand."

She was in the doorway now. "You loved it."

"Damn right. Look where it got me."

Bay blew him a kiss. Look where it got me, she thought. I'm up to my ears in emotional upheaval, personal tragedies and self-analysis. She went back to the kitchen and gathered her things.

The smell of barbecue drifting in the open window reminded her of countless summer nights in the Cove and winter nights on the islands. She looked below, thinking of Breck and the life that had kept them together twenty-four hours a day. As if to shake her reverie, she tiptoed back to Paul, a man who gave her no more than a few hours when he could squeeze them in. Her first relationship had been a dismal failure, and she had little confidence that a second try would be any different. There was nothing to go on except the cockeyed philosophy of a handsome pediatrician who seemed to believe that she could do—or be—anything she put her mind to.

Blind faith, she thought, wanting to tell him she wasn't worthy of it, wasn't capable of sustaining that amount of trust. She watched his steady breathing.

Even when worn out by the demands of his profession, he looked confident, relaxed.

Without disturbing him, she touched his hair as an ache welled up in her chest. Her body told her what her brain still refused to acknowledge; she loved him, but worse than that, she needed him.

Saturday was hot. A steady southeast wind blew over the water, promising a weekend as perfect as the previous one had been dismal. Paul arrived at the boathouse after breakfast, dropped his change of clothes, beeper and his gorgeous self onto her bed and flexed his biceps.

"I am a new man, thanks to you."

"I'm still getting used to the old one. By the way, what were you doing at Sea Mist that night? I've meant to ask now that I know you. It seems a curious place for you to party. And you weren't, as a matter of fact."

"No? I was picking up brunettes."

"I'm serious, Paul!"

He shrugged. "I got the invitation from the committee, just like you did. I get it every other year for the Bermuda Race. This time I happened to be home, seeing my folks, so I thought 'what the hell.'" He smiled. "We working-class types like to hobnob every once in a while, brush up against the upper classes, see if the tinsel rubs off."

"Baloney! You didn't brush up against a soul. I watched every move you made."

Paul was shaking his head. "How I could have missed the molten stare of your green eyes is still a mystery."

"I was being discreet."

He gave her a little pat. "Not by the time I started to pay attention!"

"Too aggressive?" There was real doubt in her eyes.

"Have you noticed any complaints?" He began to laugh at her.

"Not lately," she admitted.

They finished the conversation on the way to the yacht club. After they'd parked and taken the launch out to the boat, they settled down to some serious sailing. It felt wonderful to be with him, to be able to use her hand and to be able to skim with the wind over the course.

Hip-to-hip they hiked against the pull of the hull. The sail was tight, and the hull sliced through the water. Bay was at the helm. "You're not out far enough," she yelled.

Paul had the sheet, controlling the sail. "I'm right where I should be. You move back!"

"No way. Pull her in. I'm losing ground." She looked up at the luff and back at her crew. Just to prove it, she pulled the line tighter, the Scot biting into the chop. A whitecap slapped against the hull, soaking Paul.

"Serves you right for bossing the captain."

"You're not about to let me forget it, either."

"Nope!" She was still looking at the boat, the course and her wind indicator. "Okay, let her out."

Paul held back as they approached the first mark, taking it cleanly to port. He looked out at the buoy and then at her. "You lost time on that one."

They came about, letting the sail snap from one side to the other, soaked and grinning, throwing commands as if they were insults and all the while sailing a perfect, imaginary race.

They sailed the basin until hunger drove them back to port. There was no longer any doubt that they made a perfect team, but when Bay pointed it out, Paul replied that he had known it all along.

They skimmed through town in the open Triumph, stopping at the fish market for steamers and at the general store for beer. It was still oppressively hot.

They stayed in their sea-salty clothes at the boathouse. Paul tossed a salad, while Bay scrubbed the clams under the faucet. She rubbed away the perspiration from her forehead with the back of her hand, smiling as his arms came around her from behind, and a kiss was planted on the back of her neck.

"Salty," Paul murmured. "You taste like the soft pretzels in Philadelphia."

She shivered, enjoying the nuzzle. "College?"

"Yup."

"Penn?" It was a logical guess, but Paul snorted.

"I'm hardly Ivy League. Temple, full scholarship."

She pivoted, hugged him and then got back to rinsing their makings for dinner. "You could pass for Ivy, if you were so inclined."

"Maybe from all those years of trying to compete with Breck."

His comment made her look at him. "Breck's not Ivy, either. What do you care, anyway."

"I don't," Paul answered. "With his bucks, he doesn't need it."

"And you do? Come on, Paul, I really don't want to spend our one night together discussing my ex-husband. Temple seems to have prepared you well, and Tufts Medical School is nothing to sneeze at, you know."

He was looking at her closely. "How'd you know I went to Tufts?"

She shot him a grin. "I read your diploma in the office the morning you stitched me up. I was trying to concentrate on something besides the way I felt when you touched me." His expression softened, and she kissed him. "I'd been trying to convince myself that the man doing the sewing couldn't possibly be who I thought he was."

"But he was," he said.

She was still grinning. "Sometimes I get lucky."

When the clams had been steamed, the butter melted and the salad dressed, they carried it all in the dusk across the Chandler lawn to the beach. The ebbing tide left behind a stretch of damp sand, the last of the mating horseshoe crabs and strings of kelp.

They settled against the rocks.

"It'll be good to have my family back," Bay said between dipping and chewing the clams. She looked at the distant lights that had been turned on at dusk by Jeremy's timers. "All this solitude has been hard to take."

Paul took a swallow of beer. "Did that surprise you?"

She nodded. "I thought I needed to be alone, to sort things out, and I might have, if you hadn't dragged me off the Cliff Walk."

Paul's shadowed face came back to her. "Is that a compliment?"

Bay looked at him. "I don't know, maybe. You sure give me more to think about." Before he could comment, she leaned forward and put her fingers on his lips. "Don't get philosophical on me. It's too hot, and I'm too sticky and full."

"And happy," he added, not making it sound like a question at all.

She stood up. "The man knows me too well."

He joined her. "What do you say to a little spontaneity?" His hands were already on his shirt buttons.

"Skinny-dipping! You're brilliant! And not even Ivy League."

He growled, but kept stripping while she did the same, peeling off her sailing clothes. "Forget what I said about my family, for the moment, anyway. Feast your eyes," she cried, laughing, giving him her best shimmy in the moonlight. She shook her head. "Where are bouncy, big boobs when you need them?"

Paul laughed hard and raced her to the water. "You don't need them!" he yelled as they tumbled and tangled in the water.

He swam with sure, powerful strokes, and when he came back, she was shivering in earnest. "Damned New England water. Where's the Caribbean when you need it?"

"You've gone soft," Paul said, pressing his soaking body against her then looking down. "You're warm!"

"On the inside, maybe."

"From watching my perfect body?" he asked.

She looked disgusted. "I like a man who's shy, a certain humility..."

It was as far as she got before he scooped her up in his arms, one under her knees, the other across her back. "I've always wanted to do this," he said, carrying her back to the lawn.

Bay wrapped her arms around his neck, kissing the droplets of seawater. "Gee, in the movies it never looked like it was any effort."

Paul groaned as he dropped her gently onto the grass. "So much for my impression of Burt Lancaster," he said. "You're a lot more solid than you look."

She smiled sweetly, keeping her hands busy. "Diplomatic choice of words. Deborah Kerr wasn't carried, not that I can recall."

He stretched out beside her and guided her hand and then moved his along her thigh. "Deborah and Burt also stayed on the sand. Hollywood doesn't tell you that one grain of that stuff can turn ecstasy to torture."

Bay laughed softly, aroused, exhilarated by every aspect of him. His wit, his unconscious charm were as sexy as his body, which now ignited her by moving to within millimeters of her overheated skin.

"Take me!" she cried with all the melodrama she could muster. "From here to eternity."

He did.

Hours later when the had showered, dried, argued, laughed and made love again—this time in the brass bed—Bay lay in the dark, drifting into the most contented sleep she had ever known. She was on her side, her open palm over the steady heartbeat beneath his muscled chest.

He raised her hand and kissed it.

"You do good work," she said sleepily.

"I loved you even then, Whitney Bay, named for a deserted beach."

She let the moment float, savoring her contentment. "Paul?"

"Mmm?"

"I love you, too."

She felt his sigh and felt his cheek brush against hers.

"Bay, you'll never regret it, and some day, I promise you, we'll put away the pills and make our own babies on our own deserted beach."

He was quiet then, as if measuring her response. "Yes," she replied, "and we can name them Massachusetts Bay and Alden's Cove."

Nine

Sunday morning was everything the previous one hadn't been. A stiff, steady breeze—southeast and right off the water—blew back the organdy curtains, and what clouds there were, floated high and harmless.

But more to the point, on this Sunday morning Bay lay snuggled in Paul's arms. "You stayed," she said by way of "good morning."

"I did, didn't I?" He kissed her shoulder. "I'll try not to make a habit of it."

She snorted and hit him with a pillow. The conversation began to drift toward the day's races, boats and strategy, and while it was centered in the present, it had an air of the future about it. Contentment washed over her.

They got out of bed together, dressing for the race and the fair weather, made breakfast and settled on the deck. Bay was halfway through her honeydew melon when her eyes caught the familiar lines of a Morgan at anchor.

With her mouth full, she squinted, got to her feet and went to the rail. Paul watched her and finally offered the binoculars she kept in the living room. She put them to her eyes and swallowed.

"It can't be," she said, knowing full well that it could.

She lowered the glasses and looked at Paul. "The *Respite*'s on a guest mooring in front of the yacht club. Our boat," she added, although Paul knew full well whose it was. Her stomach was queasy.

"Do you want to faint in my arms?" Paul asked, looking smug.

"Be serious."

"Bay, your expression is serious enough for both of us. I have no idea how you want me to react to this. You look surprised, to say the least."

"Well, wouldn't you be? Good Lord, Paul! My ex-husband and our boat are right out there under my nose. Our noses."

"Did you think he'd stay in St. Thomas for the summer?"

She shook her head. "No, actually I knew he'd be in Newport for the season. I just didn't expect him here. Not now, not today..." Not when I finally begin to enjoy myself, she acknowledged to herself.

Paul pulled her into his arms and twined his fingers in her fine curls. "Are you still in love with him?" he asked quietly.

She shook her head against his chest. "Not even a little bit."

"Then this should be no different than when you'd run into him in the islands, or in Newport."

"Paul, he didn't just float into the basin by accident. This isn't Bailey's Beach—he's two days from Newport. He could at least have radioed—not that it would have occurred to him."

"You seem to be assuming he's here to see you."

She pushed away from his embrace. "Can you think of another reason?"

"Maybe he's got a charter here."

"Paul, people go to the boat; the boat doesn't go to the people."

He smiled at her. "Except in this case."

She nodded. "He's got something up his sleeve, and he's just going to sit out there until I make the first move."

Paul picked up the glasses. "You're right!" he cried. "I can see him on the bow. He's watching us with a pair of these. I can read his lips, Bay. He's saying 'Well, I'll be damned, old Whitney and the hired help!'"

She yanked the binoculars from him. "You're making me feel very foolish."

"I hope so, love. You've got more important things to stew about than an ex-husband in a boat that had cost more than my medical education."

Bay agreed, finished her meal and worked at not glancing back every ten minutes.

They set off for the regatta with time to spare, and once they were at the yacht club took the time to mingle with the other Scot contenders. Most knew either Paul or Bay; many knew both of them. It was not nearly as difficult as their first dinner at Wingate's Galley had been. She was getting used to being seen with him. It was a feeling she enjoyed.

They walked through the clubhouse and came through the double screen doors, shoulder-to-shoulder,

onto the veranda overlooking the water. Breck Scofield, a beer in his hand, was leaning against the post.
"Hello, Whit!" he said, as though he'd been waiting for
them, glancing not at her but at Paul. He extended his
hand to Paul.

"I saw your name on the manifest board as Bay's
crew and had to stick around to see if it could be the
same Bendette."

"The same," Paul said amicably.

"How you been?"

Paul smiled. "Great."

Breck, who was a hair shorter and a shade darker
than Paul, looked back at Bay. "Small world. Paul and
I—"

"I know," she interrupted. Both men looked dis-
gustingly relaxed.

"Well, you'll make a great team out there."

Her tension softened at his sincerity. "Thanks." She
looked at Breck. "*Respite* all right?"

He nodded. "She's fine. Don't let me interrupt."

Paul and Bay moved away from him, and then,
struck with an afterthought, Bay turned back. "What
are you doing in the Cove?"

He raised his beer. "I've got a proposition, but it can
wait. Give 'em hell out there, first."

Short and sweet, probably less than a minute or
two... She took Paul's arm, looking up into his handsome face, and caught a shadow of tension along his
jaw before he smiled. "You okay?" he said.

She nodded. "I love you."

An hour later, hiking off the port side of the Scot,
Bay Chandler was giving no thought to whom she
loved. Her eyes were on the red hull of her nearest con-

tender as her weight and that of Paul's pulled her own boat from a near collision.

"Head up!" she yelled. "They're stealing our wind. Head up."

Bay inched the Scot ahead, taking chances where the others didn't. At the mark they came about, and Paul ducked, moving with her as if their movements had been choreographed. It was the precision they needed to pull out. They reached the downwind leg with Paul at the helm, while Bay threw out the spinnaker and then joined him. She took a moment to enjoy the beauty of the multicolored sails that popped open around her one after the other.

Running before the wind, the fleet plowed for home with the Chandler Scot leading the pack. She looked at Paul, who was thoroughly enjoying himself, and marveled at the chances he had taken to bring them ahead. Like Bay, he had a yellow foul-weather slicker over his polo shirt and his hair and face were plastered with sea spray. He was grinning.

"You seem to have wound up at the helm, Bendette."

"So I did. Grab that buoy, will you?" He indicated the Chandler mooring. "As soon as we get the spinnaker down."

She did as she was told, furling the front, ballooned nylon as it lost the wind and deflated. Once her float was through the chock and cleated, the two of them brought down the remaining sails, secured the mainsail to the mast and stowed the jib and spinnaker. "You're so efficient," Paul quipped.

"Put us in first place, didn't it?" she said with a smirk.

They got back to the boathouse after talking shop on the veranda with the other contenders. There would be protests, but it was clear that Paul and Bay were in first place at the end of the first day's competition.

She looked out once to the *Respite*, its fifty-odd feet dwarfing many of the boats around it, and tightened her grip on Paul's arm. He had little more than an hour before he was due back at Plymouth General Hospital, an hour they filled at the boathouse with taking showers and eating an easy supper. "Will I ever have this much time with you again?" she asked over a forkful of peas.

He touched her cheek. "Even this wasn't enough." There was a pause and then he grew serious. "Bay, darling, will you come to the hospital tomorrow and see a patient of one of my colleagues?"

She looked into the depth of his eyes, seeing her own reflection and then the intensity of the man who loved her. She nodded. "For you."

"Not for me, for her and for you."

Bay looked at him sideways. "I don't suppose you waited until the last minute to ask because you were so sure I'd say yes?"

"Oh that I'd know you that well! I just wanted to avoid an argument in case you turned me down."

She touched his arm. "We argued the entire regatta—hardly the same, though, is it?"

"Hardly," he added.

They agreed on nine the following morning, but when Bay suggested that she bring Audrey Parker along, Paul asked her to wait. "This was a high-risk pregnancy all the way along. Her obstetrician had her prepared for the possibility of not making it to term. You talk with her first, then get her together with Audrey, if you think it would be beneficial."

"Use my own judgment?"

He kissed her. "You got it. And Bay?"

"There's more?"

Paul nodded. "Square things with Breck."

She drew her head back, ignoring a jolt of anxiety. "We squared things years ago, two years ago, to be precise. Whatever he wants is business. Go to the hospital and work your magic. It's you I love."

Paul gave her a final kiss. "Your taste in men is improving."

When the phone rang at seven, she expected it would be Paul, calling from the doctors' lounge. She envisioned him in a white physician's jacket, a stethoscope around his neck, and her voice was soft with desire when she said "hello."

"Whit, it's Breck."

She cleared her throat.

"Any chance you can come on the boat for a while?" When she didn't answer, he added, "*Respite*'s crawling with people. We wouldn't be alone."

She sighed. "You didn't have to say that."

"I know, but I need to see you. I want to talk about the boat, her future, and mine for that matter. Come on out. I'd come and get you, but I haven't got a car. Of course if Paul's there, it can wait."

"He's not." She hesitated. Get it over with, she told herself. They were still business partners, after all. "Okay. I'll drive out."

Forty-five minutes later, after a drive to the yacht club, the trip in the launch and a "welcome aboard,"

Bay sat on the familiar blue cushions of the open cockpit, sipping a gin and tonic.

The first mate, a Jamaican named George, was a familiar face. She shook his hand happily and then was introduced to Breck's cook, a sea-toughened character named Spoons, who looked like Willie Nelson, complete with bandanna.

The surprise was a stunning blonde, Marcia Jensen, a woman in her mid-thirties. She and Spoons were recent additions, and after the introductions all three crew members left Breck and Bay to themselves. Bay crossed her legs and tried to relax; Breck lounged next to her, his sockless Topsiders propped on the teak-trimmed banquettes. He needed a haircut.

He asked the requisite questions about her family, Jeremy's luck in the Bermuda Race and her standing in the Scot Series.

"Here's the deal," he said finally, bringing his jeans-covered legs back down and sitting up straight. "I want to add another Morgan and incorporate. I've got a guy named Matt Preston very interested. He hasn't got a lot of money to invest, but he's damned good at the wheel. He'd make a perfect captain—"

Bay was smiling. "I know Matt Preston. I ran into him during Race Week in Antigua two months ago."

Breck's eyebrows arched. "Great! My proposition is that you captain or take him on as one. Either way, we double-charter. We could tandem or run them independently. I've got the bank interested—"

"With the *Respite* as collateral?" she asked.

He nodded. "But there's no loan without you."

Bay listened and watched his enthusiasm, waiting for some twinge of regret or desire or even anxiety. There was nothing, only genuine curiosity at his suggestions.

"Come back, Whit. I know we didn't work out, but there's no reason why you should give up everything else. You're still the best captain and business partner I ever had."

She smiled. "Thanks, but I'm not there anymore. I don't belong in St. Thomas, not like you do."

"Hell," he said, "you haven't been gone more than a month. This isn't a whim; it's my future."

She measured her words. "For you, Breck, you're right. But it was a whim for me. There was no future in it for me, and you saw that as well as I did. It was one of our biggest problems."

He let her talk and then leaned back. "It's Bendette, isn't it?"

Their eyes met, hers hazel, his brown. "Not completely. I needed to come home and sort things out, make my own future. Paul's got me doing more than sailing; he got me facing myself—pushing me almost." She stopped as the old familiar lump pressed against her breastbone. "I'm doing some counseling with women who have had miscarriages."

Breck's eyes widened. "Christ, why dredge all that up?"

The Scofield approach to life, she thought.

"Put it behind you, Whitney. You're in love with him, aren't you?"

She sipped the drink. "Are you letting him do this to you?" he added.

"Breck, that's enough!" she finally said.

He nodded in agreement. "Okay, I'll back off. Think about my offer, though. I'll be in Newport all summer; there's no need for a decision until September, anyway." He took the airhorn and gave the short blasts that would call back the launch. Bay got up.

"How long will you be in the Cove, Breck?"

He jammed his hands into his hip pockets. "Awhile. I've got day trips lined up along the north of the Cape, here to Provincetown. I'll be in and out this week, anyway. If you need me, I'll be right here."

Bay smiled. "I don't need you." Not anymore, she knew. In a quieter voice she asked about Marcia Jensen. "A recent addition?"

He grinned. "Yeah. Met her in Tortola. She's from San Diego originally... good for me."

Meaning she doesn't ask anything of you, Bay thought. He was studying her. "Is there something else?" she asked.

"Damn it, there is. I've hurt you enough, I think. We did quite a number on each other. I don't want you to go through that with Paul."

His honesty surprised her, and she let him continue. "You're a great kid, whether we made it or not. Paul and I are old rivals." He hesitated. "Maybe you should know. Sailing, tennis, a couple of women way back. I stole a girl from him when he was in college and I wasn't even out of boarding school. Summer romance... She took one look at my car, my club, and Bendette didn't stand a chance. Stupid, half-assed thing to do."

"You never mentioned it, or him, for that matter."

He shrugged. "Never gave it any thought till now. I was a kid, and she was the older woman, all of nineteen, I think. Good old Sheila Dunlap. Who knows what happened to her?" He looked closely at Bay. "I want to make sure there's no revenge left in him."

"That was a long time ago," she said quietly, more to herself than to Breck.

Bay got home after dark, trying to concentrate on Breck's business venture. She and Breck were co-owners of the *Respite*, and her own reluctance did not seem reason enough to keep him from developing what for Breck could be a real career with enormous potential. Her family would be home soon: sound business advice as close as the neighboring houses.

Paul had begun to fill the void she had felt in their absence, and she lay on her back in the dark, thinking about Breck's story and the fact that after all those years the pediatrician still had Sheila Dunlap's photo stuck in his mirror.

She rolled over and called the hospital, and had him paged. She was told he didn't pick it up, and after a four-minute wait, she hung up. Her sleep was fitful.

When Paul did call, it was from home, at seven in the morning, and the offer was for breakfast. She accepted.

Her appetite was minimal, as she suffered equal parts anxiety over the waiting patient and Breck's conversation. She told Paul about Breck's plans for the *Respite*. She finished with a shrug. "He seems to have it all worked out." She omitted any mention of former romances.

"And it hinges on you?"

"My signature, at least. If I know my family, they'll encourage it as a good investment financially, anyway."

"Rather than emotionally?"

Bay smiled. "Precisely."

Paul studied her face. "You wouldn't want to captain the second one?"

"Not in the Caribbean. I have other things to do now." He seemed relieved, but it could have been her imagination. After finishing the muffins and coffee, they left for the hospital in separate cars.

Once they arrived at the hospital, Paul walked her to the nurses' station on the Maternity/Gynecology floor and had the obstetrician paged. He kissed her lightly only to have a nurse wink and say, "It's about time he got around to a little recreation."

Bay laughed and turned her attention to the approaching doctor, a Plymouth OB named Jane Crandall. They walked the corridor together. "Paul and I have discussed this so often," she was saying. "Some sort of support group is badly needed, Bay. If you decide to continue, I'll give you all the advice and support I can. Paul tells me you were a great help with one of his referrals from Alden's Cove."

Bay smiled. "I tried. It did seem to make a difference. The best part is that I made a friend in the bargain."

The doctor patted her arm. "That's one of the biggest benefits, to cut through the sense of isolation. On top of grief, it can be overwhelming."

They reached the private room and walked together to the bedside. A woman in her mid-thirties was watching television, her knees drawn up. Her hair was freshly brushed, but she lacked any sign of makeup or enthusiasm.

Bay looked from her placid face back to Jane Crandall. "Mrs. Stavos, this is Bay Chandler, the woman I was telling you about. Bay, Anita Stavos."

The woman tugged at her sheet. "Dr. Crandall, I've changed my mind. I'm not ready. I really don't want to talk to no one." She looked at Bay. "I don't see what you can do."

Her doctor nodded, still in the process of pulling up a chair. "Perhaps Bay could just sit with you, then."

There was a reluctant nod, and the doctor left the women alone.

Bay sat down facing Anita, waiting for a sign, a hint as to her disposition. She touched the woman's wrist, her own fingers cold from apprehension. The television continued to drone, and the woman stared at it.

"There's nothing you can do," she said to the screen. "It don't matter now—"

"I know how overwhelming the loss is," Bay answered, keeping her voice steady but raising it so she could be heard over the quiz game. A buzzer was sounding behind a gameboard and her irritation mounted.

She tried to take her cues from Anita, which was difficult since the woman continued to stare at the screen. She had not, however, pulled her hand back. Bay thought about Audrey Parker and the inroads she had made, the comfort and the assurances she had gained.

"It's not your fault," she said at last. "I'm sure Dr. Crandall has told you that."

The woman's eyes finally left the set. On-screen, bells were ringing as the audience yelled encouragement. "Not my fault? You tell my husband. You tell his parents! I lost a son."

"Anita! It wasn't something *you* did."

"I danced at my sister's wedding."

Bay's fingers tightened. "Surely Dr. Crandall—"

"Dr. Crandall, you...I don't need a kid like you telling me not to blame myself."

Bay's heart skipped a beat. "Anita—"

"No!" came out as a shout and the woman clapped her hands over her ears. On the television the game was over, and the credits were running to the sounds of clapping and cheering. "It took me four years to get

pregnant, and now it's gone. I'm nearly forty, not like
you...."

Bay sat frozen, wanting to say there could be another chance, wanting to be the chirpy little optimist
and tell this woman she could do anything she put her
mind to. *Lies.* Life didn't work that way, did it? Not for
Bay, not for Anita.

The woman was crumpling in front of her, driven
further into her grief by the fact that Bay sat there reminding her of it. Bay wanted to be forty, then, wanted
to be a blue-collar wife with superstitious in-laws so she
could be proof that there was hope. Instead she offered
a tissue.

"Please, Anita, your husband will understand in
time—" Maybe that was a lie, too, for all she knew. It
was as far as she got before a crisp-looking, irritated
nurse appeared at the door. "What's going on here?"

Bay stood up. "Dr. Crandall suggested that I might
help Mrs. Stavos...." Her explanation sounded as weak
as it was.

The nurse looked at her watch and then at Bay. "As
you can see, you've managed to make things worse.
Mrs. Stavos has requested no visitors. Had I
known—"

"It had been cleared with her physician," Bay said in
defense.

"Doctors don't always know what's best for their
patients, as you can see. You had better leave."

Bay looked at Anita, who was sobbing openly now,
jamming the tissue to her swollen eyes. Bay left the
room without looking back.

Ten

Without a word she turned in the hall toward the bank of elevators, leaving the patient to the nurse. Paul would be with patients or colleagues; she was not about to break down in front of them.

She felt useless. More than useless, disruptive. Anguish tied her in knots as she drove home with the mental picture of Anita Stavos's despair. Failure hung on her like the fog that was now shrouding the harbor. The visibility diminished even while she picked at her lunch. Pacing was not her style, but she did that, too, looking from her deck to the Chandler grounds, as empty as her emotions.

She tried Audrey Parker but got no answer. Then she went into the bedroom, pulling off her dress along the way. She replaced it with jeans and a polo shirt, stuffed her foul-weather gear in a canvas bag, and slamming into Jeremy's car, she threw it into reverse. For the first time since her teenage rebellion, Bay Chandler left twenty feet of skid marks in the gravel of her father's driveway.

The launch took her to the *Scot* while she studied the weather. Small Craft Warnings had not been posted, so the wind was not quite as stiff as she had thought. Even if they had been, they were for sailors' discretion. It was up to her judgment, she thought. Well, damn it, when it came to water and weather, her judgment was impeccable.

There was just enough visibility to sail the basin. She intended to keep in sight of the land, and when the launch nosed up to the hull of the *Scot*, she thanked the driver and scrambled aboard.

Her judgment told her not to hoist the jib. Concentrating on the single mainsail would be work enough. Though there was no competition, barely another boat under sail in the heavy weather, she kept the Scot close-hauled, sailing at breakneck speed through the choppy waters, with the expertise that came from a lifetime of practice. She whooped and hollered, keeping the sail in tight with her gloved hand, pressing her weight on the centerboard trunk with her boat shoe.

The concentration kept her from thinking of anything except her course and the wind and the constant soaking she got from the spray. The physical surge of confidence was as exhilarating as the wind.

However, once her course was set, her mind began to wander. She saw Anita Stavos's face when she looked up at the sail and thought of her words as she tacked across the channel.

The fury and frustration of carrying the responsibility for something beyond her control tore at her heart.

It kindled emotions so close to Anita's that even as she checked her course, her eyes filled and she began to cry.

Out there alone in the chop with the wind and the circling gulls, Bay did all the right moves by instinct. She moved the boat as if it were an extension of herself. When a wind shift threatened her course, she executed a perfect jibe and sat back down.

"Damn!" she yelled into the wind. "Damn you, Paul, damn you, Jeremy, damn Dr. Crandall!" She had tampered with someone's emotional stability and now had to fight for her own.

Back and forth, back and forth, she tacked until her energy and frustration had been expended. After more than an hour's hard work, she brought the boat about and headed back down the channel toward the basin. With the sail fully out and the centerboard adjusted, she relaxed. Time and tide, she thought, time and tide.

Bay didn't see another soul until she was back among the anchored boats. She slipped through the moorings, darting around the deep-water yachts. The *Respite* still sat at the guest mooring, looming out of the fog. Breck was standing on the bow, waving.

On a whim she brought the *Scot* as close to the Morgan as she dared, sliding along the length of her while Breck whistled and told her she looked fantastic. She kept going, sliding back out to her own buoy, and with the sails luffing into the wind, she pulled up her mooring and secured the boat.

When the sails were secured, she called for the launch. She realized once they were underway that the taxi service was also picking up those aboard the *Respite*.

Breck and Marcia got into the launch, waved off by George and Spoons. They each carried a duffel bag.

"Good sail?" Marcia asked.

"Cathartic," Bay answered.

Breck's eyes were on her. "You were something to see," he added. "Always have been."

Marcia looked at him sideways, and he put his hand on her knee. "We're off to Boston to see some old friends of Marcia's and pick up some supplies."

Bay looked at the other woman. "I hope you'll take some time to sightsee."

Marcia nodded. "I want to take it all in. I've never been east, except to the islands, of course."

"Of course," Bay answered. "Do you two need a lift somewhere?"

Breck shook his head. "I rented a car from the corner gas station."

Bay nodded. "Then I guess you're all set. Enjoy yourselves."

The highlight of the day, her family's return, had nearly been put out of her head. They were due by dark, Bay thought as she looked at the gray sky, provided the weather improved.

Her phone was ringing as she climbed the stairs, and she got it after dropping the canvas on the deck. It was Paul, his voice full of business. "Darling, I've been calling since this morning."

"I've been sailing."

"I thought you might be. How are you?"

Bay studied the horizon through the window. "All right, considering."

"You should have had me paged. I talked with Jane Crandall—"

"What good would it have done? The damage won't be repaired by my running to you. Besides, you were busy."

She could hear his steady breathing.

"Bay, stop implying that I'm insensitive."

"Insensitive? I would have said misguided. I made a mess of everything." Her voice caught. "I did more harm than good. This wasn't some damned regatta. Anita Stavos is worse today, thanks to me, than she was yesterday."

"Bay, don't be so hard on yourself," Paul said quietly.

His soothing voice, usually so stimulating, deepened her anger. "Hard on myself! And what do you think I was on her? I tampered with someone. I had no right and no expertise." She was gripping the phone.

"Bay, love, think what you've meant to Audrey Parker, what a difference you've made. Every case is different. You can't always be one hundred percent successful."

"Tell Anita that!"

"And sometimes," he continued, "the good comes later. Once she's had time to digest it all. I've seen her, by the way. She's shaken but fine—better, in fact."

"Better?" Bay repeated. "That doesn't surprise me. After one session with me, she had no place to go but up."

"Bay—"

"Paul, we're getting nowhere. My parents are due back tonight, and I have other things to think about." She wanted to add that other things helped to keep her from dwelling on the trauma, but she knew that would stir up more comment, more pressure, and that was the one thing she didn't need.

"I can't live up to your expectations," she said in a dead voice.

"Which are?"

She chewed her lip. "The expectation that if you push hard enough I'll turn into what you want me to be. I'll be reborn as someone breezing through life making things better for people."

"You do."

"Well, I sure as hell didn't today."

She heard him sigh into the receiver and then heard the beeper paging him. There was a low obscenity. "None of this can be resolved over the phone. Will you come over tonight? We need to talk."

"I can't. My family—"

"Of course," he said, not making it sound sarcastic. "Make time for me. It's important."

"*Me* make time for you?"

"Soon."

"I'll try," she said, and they hung up.

The ground fog began to lift, even if her spirits didn't. She called the airport and was told arrivals were on time at Logan. Somebody's timing is right, anyway, she thought.

She ate dinner alone, undisturbed by anything until a car horn sounded at the top of the lane at eight. The Chandlers had arrived. Bay, in shorts and a blouse, walked and then ran up the gravel to the Big House, where two airport limousines were spilling baggage and people from every door.

She hugged them all, her brothers, their wives, her nephews, her niece and then her parents. Her delight was genuine, and her spirits lifted.

"What's this?" her father asked, wiping a tear from her cheek.

"I missed you."

His hug was tight, tighter than usual. With the exception of Jeremy, she had not seen any of them since the previous Christmas holidays. The look that passed between her and Jeremy lacked any of the defiance of their night at Sea Mist.

Her mother hugged her as she said, "Darling, I hope you're home for good." The others asked her how the Cove seemed after all that time. She answered that it seemed wonderful, which was mostly true, and that they looked wonderful, which was entirely true.

All but her parents piled back into the cars for the drive to the bordering houses, and she followed her mother and father into their kitchen.

"Jeremy tells us you've met Paul Bendette."

Bay's heart jumped. "He's crewing for me."

They were pleased and waited tactfully for more information. She was surprised at her own reluctance, at the turbulence still brewing inside her. Instead she asked about her Bermudian cousins and steered the conversation around them and the race, even sailmaking.

Within half an hour the rest of the family had changed and returned, and they all settled on the wicker-filled porch to catch the breeze. There were still no stars, but the weather had lifted.

"*Respite*'s in the harbor," Bay said finally. Six sets of adults' eyes looked at her.

"With Breck?" asked Christopher.

She nodded and told them of his proposition. They listened.

"You wouldn't go back?" That was from her mother, and Bay shook her head. "This Matt Preston would sail it for you, in other words."

Bay nodded. "It would be strictly an investment."

John Chandler sipped his iced tea. "Frankly, I wouldn't mind seeing my daughter investing wisely." He meant that it was about time, she was sure. "I think you should give it some thought."

"I am." Hearing herself say it made her realize that she was.

Jeremy behaved himself and did not bring up the subject of Paul Bendette until Bay started for her own apartment. He insisted on accompanying her. "You've got a lot to think about, Kiddo," he said for openers.

She nodded. "It's not the easiest thing in the world, trusting Breck's judgment. That's why I need your opinions on this deal."

"He knows boats, he knows sailors and he's got the capital." Jeremy paused and looked at her. "This keeps you tied to him in a way. Have you thought about that?"

"Yes."

"And?"

She smiled. "No pings, no pangs. Besides, he's found someone else. She's nice, actually. Marcia something."

"And you?"

They had reached the boathouse. "Dad's already asked me about my crew, if that's what you mean."

Jeremy smiled. "That's what I mean."

Bay looked at her brother. "Equal parts ping and pang at the moment."

They separated, and he started back to the Big House, his hands in his pockets. "True love runs a rocky road," he called.

She wanted to tell him she'd had more than her share of potholes, but Bay kept her doubts to herself.

When the phone rang, she was already dressed for bed and staring at herself in the mirror over her bathroom vanity. Staring as if the reflected image were a stranger, one who would start talking and tell her what to do with her life.

"Well." She looked at the glass, repeating her brother's words. "Are you going to get your act together? Everybody's watching now, Kiddo." She flicked off the light and went to pick up the bedside phone.

The voice was familiar but unexpected. "It's Breck," he said. "I've been calling all night. Just get in with Paul?"

"I've been at the Big House. My family just got back." Paul was none of his business.

"Great. Tell them I said hello. Did you happen to mention my business venture?"

"As a matter of fact, I did. Breck, can't this wait? I'm very tired—"

"Sure, sure," he agreed hastily. "I know it's late. I'm in a bind and I need you."

"Where are you?"

"I'm in Boston, still. I need you tomorrow. Marcia wants to stay here, see her friends and all, and I've got a charter tomorrow morning, a quick cruise to Provincetown and back."

"And you want me to crew in Marcia's place?"

"Whit, these guys have no interest in sailing, they want to be sailed. They don't sail, as a matter of fact. I need an extra hand. What do you say?"

"How long?" She knew the answer before she asked.

"Two days." There was a pause. "Marcia approves."

Bay wanted to say that she'd never known him to need anyone's approval, but she didn't.

"Come on," he urged her. "Go for it. The weather's supposed to be great; full day out, full day back. We'll beach wherever it looks good."

She was nodding silently as he talked; a sense of relief at no longer being part of his life washed over her. Glamour was in the eyes of the beholder, she thought, delighted that none of this seemed more than commonplace. It gave her the gumption to say yes.

"Hot damn," he said. "I'm driving back soon. I'll see you on the *Respite* at eight, okay?"

"Okay."

Before she had time to change her mind, she hung up and tapped Paul's number, letting it ring until he answered. His voice was thick with sleep.

"Paul," she said, "I'm sorry to wake you."

"Bay? What time is it?"

"Late. Nearly midnight, but I thought you should know that I'm taking my boat out tomorrow for two days. I need some time and—"

"The Scot? Where are you going?" He sounded suddenly awake.

Her heart began to race. "Not the Scot. I'm crewing on the *Respite*, just to P-town and back."

"Just to P-town." Very awake.

She cleared her throat. "I'm half-owner, you know, and Breck's in a bind—"

"I know damn well what you are, and what you are to the captain."

That was followed by a thick silence, broken by Bay. "This is nothing more than a business venture. Forty-eight hours."

"And when the going gets tough, it's a lot easier to ship out than to stick around and—"

"That's enough! I'm not running away from anything. My little career in the maternity ward is over. It
ended with Anita. I know where my skills lie, Paul. I
know what I do well and what I am a dismal failure at.
Breck knows, too, even if you don't."

She regretted the final outburst the minute she'd finished, but part of her knew it was the truth and that he
should hear it. "I can't be what you want, Paul. Maybe
we both can do some thinking while I'm away."

She had listened to herself, listened to the truth that
had come out so unexpectedly. "You're so busy you'll
probably not even know I'm gone."

"Don't count on it."

"Well, I'll miss you, just as I always do."

"Do what you have to do," he said after another long
pause.

"That's it?" she asked quietly.

"That's it."

Eleven

Bay awoke at six-thirty to the froggy blast of the fog-horn on the jetty at the mouth of the harbor. The mist was light, an indication that fair weather lay above the low cover and would appear as soon as the fog burned off.

She dressed for the boat, packed a simple duffel bag, slung her foul-weather gear over her shoulder and locked the boathouse. She announced herself at the Big House, explained what she was up to and begged a ride from her father.

There were arched eyebrows; she was very used to arched eyebrows.

She wound up riding with Christopher and her father, and Jeremy scooted by in the Triumph. They let her off at the yacht-club lot, but not before John Chandler brought up the subject of gainful employment. "With us," he added, as if the subject had not been broached a million times.

This time she didn't automatically refuse. "I'm giving it some thought," she said, raising eyebrows again. "I don't know. If I'm home to stay, it seems logical. I have to do something." She blew them a kiss by way of a thank-you and eased from the car before there was time for more discussion.

The air-conditioned car had the windows up, and she was just as glad she couldn't hear the comments of one Chandler to another.

She watched the Mercedes-Benz wheel back out to the village street, and then she turned for the pier and the launch. Within fifteen minutes she was seated, again, on the cockpit cushions of the *Respite*. She took a mug of coffee from Spoons, who had a bandanna around his forehead and on his biceps a tattoo that said *Shirley*. George gave her a cheery nod and looked at Breck.

"Hey, Mon," he said in his thick Jamaican English, "she's burnin' off. Be gone by nine."

"And so will we," Breck answered, indicating the open charts on the table in the galley. "Take a look," he added to Bay. "I need your advice."

She tossed the duffel bag into the fo'c'sle, the forwardmost cabin hung with hammocks reserved for crew, and thought about how strange it would feel to sleep that night in the netting. Strange and good. Her last free-lance captain's position had included a real berth, her first aboard any boat under her charge.

She came back out to the table and sat, watching Breck's finger trace their route, a simple one along the north coast of Cape Cod. Queen Anne Island by four that afternoon and Provincetown by sunset, was what he anticipated, and Bay agreed that it could easily be done with a steady wind.

He folded the charts in order, leaving Alden's Cove to the Cape Cod Canal open, next to the wheel. Bay thought to ask if he'd requested a mooring, and he nodded. "Newport Yacht Club gets you a lot of places," he quipped.

She watched his smirk, liking it even less than she had three years earlier. She finished her coffee and took the mug to Spoons, thinking about the fact that the very attributes that made her ex-husband a strong captain on water could make him insufferable on land. Why hadn't she seen that when it really mattered? She returned, shaking her head.

He was coiling a line. "Paul upset with you?"

She bristled. "I don't need his permission to sail."

"Not even with me?"

She turned so suddenly that she nearly lost her balance. "Wait a minute! Did you set this up to get at him?" Her eyes were wide, and anger rose in her chest. "What the hell has he ever done—"

Breck laughed, holding his hand up. "I'm innocent, I swear. Calm down. I just know how the guy thinks. I'm surprised *he* didn't mention it."

Bay did nothing to hide her disgust. "Paul Bendette is neither vindictive nor childish. You and I are business partners, and he knows it. That's all this is, Breck. If you two have some old unsettled score, you'd better think twice about using me to settle it." She looked from him to the launch, approaching with two couples and a pile of luggage. They looked like the picture of a liquor advertisement's idea of yachting. Here we go, Bay realized.

She looked once more at Breck. "Turn your charm back on. Your company's arriving."

His smile was dazzling. "You know me too well."

"You're not kidding."

The sun was breaking through just as George had said it would, and Bay pulled off her fisherman's sweater and went through the boat to leave it in her hammock. If Paul suspected Breck of setting them up, he hadn't mentioned it. She thought about his voice, the fatigue and tension in it, and wondered if he had held back his apprehension. There was a stab of pure emotion—love—for his strength and his humor and his disposition, all of which were infinitely more appealing than the traits that characterized the overage preppy now charming the customers topside.

Had time numbed her so that she'd forgotten? She shook her head. Time had made her immune to Breck, that was for sure. Bay watched Breck for a minute and then smiled to herself. They could get along; they would get along and then she would go home to the man she loved.

She was introduced to Sam and Diana Clark and Howard and Susan Yacco, a foursome who made up in enthusiasm what they lacked in nautical knowledge. Bay bit back a laugh, enjoying their eagerness. There was not a stitch of anything on them that looked as if it had been worn before that morning, from khaki shirt to stiff, new leather boat shoes. She made a mental promise on the spot to see that their cruise would be a memorable one. And that Breck Scofield and her relationship with him would not mar it.

With the VHF marine radio on, the gear stowed and the enthusiasm bubbling, they set sail with Breck at the wheel, First Mate George at the halyards and Bay working the winches. Spoons did some serenading.

They killed the engine at the tip of the jetty and entered Cape Cod Bay under full sail.

At ten-fifteen she stood next to Breck, reading the chart. He asked her for a peanut-butter sandwich. "I'll take the helm," she replied. "You go see the cook about it."

Breck looked at her sideways. "I forgot. You don't do sandwiches."

She met his gaze. "I don't do sandwiches when there's a cook aboard and I'm sailing, any more than you do. You are perfectly capable of slapping some Welch's on a slab of Skippy."

Breck made a "tsk, tsk" sound. "Testy."

She smiled and retorted, "Damn right. We've fought about everything else in life; I draw the line at peanut butter and jelly."

Breck's humor was intact. "What would Annette Funicello say?"

"She'd admire your culinary ability, and I suggest we change the subject before I lose what's left of my sense of humor."

He nodded and went back to looking at the compass. Without a sandwich.

The sail was glorious. Alongshore they skirted lobstermen stringing traps and hauling trawls. There was a fishing boat or two, and larger whale-watch boats under power. The guests were thrilled by the idea of spotting whales.

By midday they reached Queen Anne Island, an uninhabited land mass off Brewster, where they anchored, swam and ate the sandwiches prepared by Spoons.

Breck was still throwing orders around that made Bay think all the more of Paul Bendette and his even temper. She missed a hundred things about him, except the pressure of living up to his expectations. Bay munched her BLT and looked at the *Respite*'s captain. Did Breck have any aspirations for her?

Life for Breck was perfect the way it was, and as long as Bay had thought so too, they'd gotten along fine. Good luck, Marcia, she thought. Beyond chartering yachts, Breck had no aspirations at all.

After lunch and a swim, they resumed their course, moving out into the bay and north toward the tip of Cape Cod. Breck had the two couples winching and adjusting the sheets while they changed tacks.

Bay, now in her bikini, came back from the bow with the communal bottle of suntan oil. She stood next to Breck. "Marcia makes peanut-butter sandwiches for you, I assume?"

He turned and looked at her. "She's a good sailor."

"Which means she takes orders?"

He shrugged, his eyes on the sail and the compass. "Better than you did, if that's what you're fishing at."

"I wasn't fishing. I'm just curious as to whom you wound up with this time."

He nodded, still keeping his eyes busy, his hands on the wheel. "I don't see it as *this time*. I'm sure that surprises you. Marcia's a little older than I am; she's been married before, too. She's had enough of it and wants no strings, wants life like I'm living it."

"How'd you get so lucky?" Bay asked. "A woman who asks no more than a beautiful sunset."

He turned this time and looked at her. "Did we hurt each other that much?" There was sincerity in his face, and he shook his head. "Was our judgment so bad that we can't get back on track? I've found what I want, Bay, and Marcia has, too. I hope you have. Paul Bendette might be it—who knows."

"Who knows," she repeated.

"He's more your style, what you should have had all along, someone with a profession, real honest-to-God ambition, as long as that ambition is not to get back at me.''

She was startled. ''Is there some sort of vendetta between you two?''

''Not as far as I'm concerned.''

His words made her heart skip. ''Breck, what are you saying? Why have you gotten me out here for two days?''

''I needed a third crew member.'' This was as far as he got before they nosed into the wind, and all hands scrambled for a chance to help bring the yacht about. Breck barked orders, which included a threat to keelhaul George for sloppiness, a threat the Yaccos and Clarks thought was hilarious.

''Yeah, Mon,'' George yelled back at him, ''I be under da boat, you be up da creek!'' It was true.

Bay gave her attention to the boat and then thought of Paul. She thought about his little patients and the hospital, about Audrey and Anita, people who struggled with the harsh realities of life. She looked at the *Respite*'s captain, who had never struggled with anything more than a recalcitrant anchor line since the day he was born.

She watched him, the sail and the wind indicator. An investment in a second yacht meant bank loans. Breck would have to be financially responsible. A second boat would put a second captain under his command, responsibility upon responsibility. Figuratively, anyway, Breck Scofield wanted to put himself in a position to go down with the ship. She thought about the venture in human terms, a chance for her to make a dream come true, certainly. But suddenly she could see the implication that it offered Breck Scofield the chance to grow up.

Which, she thought, is precisely what Paul Bendette is offering me.

The *Respite* reached the tip of Cape Cod by late afternoon, under full sail. Breck radioed the harbor master for a guest mooring and got one only because it had been reserved, and then they joined the hundreds of pleasure crafts off the shoreline. They opted for a quick trip ashore to peruse the artists' colony, to be followed by dinner.

It was old hat to Breck, Bay and the Yaccos. The Clarks begged for time, and they all wandered the streets till nine. Bay picked up a watercolor of Truro's dunes for her living room and a scrimshaw and silver bookmark for Paul. She thought about him asleep with *The New England Journal of Medicine* over his lap.

Breck, ever the captain, took two turns at rowing the crowd back to the yacht. It was dark, and the Morgan was lit now by its lamps and running lights. Spoons had a hibachi going on the stern, and fat slabs of beef waiting to sizzle.

By the time dinner was served, Bay's gaiety was forced. She wanted to be, of all places, in the sweltering apartment over the doctors' offices. She wanted to sip mediocre wine and listen to the swat of the tennis ball below and have Paul asleep in the next room, if need be. She shook her head. She had to be in love.

Bay slept, as all the crew did, cradled in the hammock in the fo'c'sle, lulled by the swaying sea beneath the *Respite* and the knowledge that she would be home in twenty-four hours.

The wind rose with the occupants the next morning, and there was a request to do "some serious sailing" on the return leg. The crew was delighted, and both Bay and George put the couples to work as they hoisted the sails and got underway.

Breck barked at everyone and everyone barked back, thoroughly enjoying themselves and the day. The course brought them due west from Provincetown, across the mouth of Cape Cod Bay so that the first land they sighted was Gurnet Point at the mouth of Plymouth Bay.

Amid the working lobster boats and returning pleasure crafts, they set anchor for the last time, enjoying the beach below the lighthouse set on the bluff.

Bay was the only one anxious to return, a fact she hid dutifully by plunging into the water with the rest of them. They lunched and fooled around and enjoyed the sun. From her towel on the bow, Bay watched a lobsterman setting traps, moving slowly through the water while the metal cages dropped, one after the other, on their trawl from the stern. She could smell the ripe bait buckets, and it reminded her of the returning boats the night she went to Wingate's Galley with Paul. Everything reminded her of Paul.

At four the *Respite* raised her sails for the last time and headed south, across Plymouth Bay and down along the coast to Alden's Cove.

The guests were the first to leave, after an hour of packing, saying goodbye and promising to hire the *Respite* in St. Thomas some winter.

Bay stayed aboard to clean up and pack her own gear. She found the captain settled back on the cushions, a beer in his hand. "Wasn't so bad, was it?"

She smiled. "I'll agree we make better partners than we ever did a couple." She watched him for a moment. "Why am I here?"

Breck was thoughtful. "I needed an extra hand."

"You could have called Jeremy, and that's just for starters."

He looked at her. "What do you think?"

She didn't like what she suspected, but she threw it out anyway. "I think that for some unknown reason it's important for you to prove to Paul Bendette that you are still capable of winning. I am getting the sickening feeling that, somehow, I'm the prize." Her eyes danced with anger, flashing as she stood glaring at him. If George and Spoons were within earshot, they had the sense to stay out of sight.

"Are you in love with him?"

"Yes." She was as taken aback by the quick response as he was. "And no matter what you think you're up to, or how this looks, I never would have come on board in the first place if I had thought there'd be a chance that Paul would misconstrue it." She sat down. "And he won't."

Breck offered her a swallow of the beer, which she took. "Well," he said, "as usual you're not far wrong."

She gasped.

"Bay, old love of mine, I've been a real bastard, I know that. I also know I've got a lot of making up to do."

"Breck—"

"Let me finish. I'm in love, too, you know, with a woman who's managed to make me see what you never could, as hard as you tried. Marcia's good for me in the same way Paul's good for you. I asked you to sail because I want to maintain our working relationship. The islands are big enough for both of us, and I hate being responsible for your giving it all up."

Bay looked at him, really looked for the first time in more than two years. Amazing, she thought, the man's apologizing! She took another swallow of the beer.

"What does this have to do with Paul?" She raised her hand. "Wait, I want to know, but it's just as important that you know I didn't run from St. Thomas because of you. I'm not a Scofield—" she patted his knee and smiled "—even though I tried. I think calling it quits was one of the few mature things I ever did. That and coming home. I belong *here*. You're the sailor, the *real* sailor and you're a good investment—while we're on the subject."

He grinned. "Thanks."

She smiled back. "I think I have a future here."

"I hope so. I just want you to be careful this time. Make sure you know what you're doing. You've been through enough; that's, I admit, a very small reason why I got you aboard. Bendette owes me more than one. I want to make damn sure he doesn't collect through you."

She was touched. "Breck, in some crazy way that was very sweet, but you two aren't kids anymore. Paul isn't collecting on any debt. He's not the type, and I'd like to think I know him better than you do."

"On that score you're probably right. You deserve better than you got the first time around."

Bay shook her head and leaned over to kiss his cheek. "So do you."

We've parted friends. She was still thinking about it long after the launch had returned her to the yacht club.

It was after dark by the time she called home, and John Chandler agreed to pick her up. When he pushed open the car door in the small lot twenty minutes later, he laughed.

"I haven't picked you up over here since you were a kid. I kind of like it."

She smiled back at him and settled into the passenger seat. "I kind of like it, too. Feels like old times, feels like home."

Her father sighed as though something long questioned might finally be answered. There was polite silence, and then she chatted about the cruise. "You know," she finished, "Breck's a good investment—as a business venture. I'm more convinced than ever."

They pulled into the compound and continued down to the boathouse. "We'll see what we can do," her father added, helping with the small duffel bag.

She rushed up the staircase to her apartment, and headed directly for the phone. It was already in her hand when she hesitated. "Do what you have to do" was how Paul had ended the last conversation. She put it down and took a shower.

Bay didn't try again until she was dry and in bed for the night. Nearly eleven was not the best time to call, and she had to grit her teeth just to punch the number. Her heart was back to its racing.

"Paul?" she said quietly after his sleepy hello. "I guess I woke you up."

"Bay," he said in a sleepy monotone. "Yes, you did. How are you?"

It was as though nothing had passed between them except her crazy behavior at Sea Mist. "Fine. I'm fine." Her stomach flipped.

"Did you do a lot of thinking? That *is* what you told me you were going to do."

"Yes," she stammered. This was worse than puberty. "I'm back and I missed you."

"I find that hard to believe."

"Paul! I admit now it looks a little crazy, but I was helping on my own boat, and I did have lots of time to think about us. Really, Paul, you're out of line, I—"

"I'm not out of line. I'm out of patience. I've done a lot of thinking, too. You get yourself into an emotional crisis, and your solution is to run away. Always, it seems, and this time to your ex-husband, no less."

Her trepidation turned to anger. "Where were you? I couldn't run to you, could I?"

There was dead silence again, and the sharp intake of breath on both ends of the line.

"I didn't mean that," she said immediately. "I don't need Breck. All I did was crew for him. He needed the help, and it gave me the chance to confirm my idea about investing in another yacht. He's in love with someone else, and so am I."

"You have a strange way of showing it."

"Not as strange as you seem to think. I know about you and Breck and the stupid rivalries. This isn't one of those. I love you, Paul. As a matter of fact, Breck was very worried that you were simply using me to get back at him after all these years."

"He would think that."

She was getting nowhere. "Well, maybe he had reason to."

"So much for trust. I think we better hang up before this whole relationship goes down the tube," he said.

There was a twenty-pound weight on her chest. "I think you are every bit as good at running away from things as I. Go back to work, run yourself into the ground, night after night. See how much good that does you and your patients. I'll see you Sunday for the race," she added, "provided it doesn't rain."

They hung up. The Good Ship Lollipop had capsized. Back to reality.

Twelve

———

She turned out the light and sat in the dark, her knees drawn up and wrapped by her arms. She stared out at the deck and the dark outline of her furniture while everything fell apart inside her.

Bay lay for a long time in the pillows, wide awake, her bed wide and empty. What finally lulled her to sleep was the imagined rocking of the hammock and the gentle movement of the *Respite* under her.

At eight the next morning she was skewering cantaloupe, sitting in her deck chair in a T-shirt and a bathing suit. There were footsteps on the gravel, which startled her, but when she saw that it was Jeremy, she decided not to give him the satisfaction of acting surprised.

"Well, hello," she said cheerfully, offering a piece of the fruit from the end of her fork. "You certainly look ready to beat back the world."

He bent his head and took off the bite and then lowered the rest of himself into an empty chair. He was in a khaki business suit, rep tie and loafers. "Care to join me at the office? Gainful employment has its advantages."

"I'm on vacation."

"With your ex-husband?"

Her eyes widened. "Of course not."

Jeremy pulled an invitation from the breast pocket of his suit. "This is for a clambake, week from Saturday. It's also my excuse to come up here and knock some sense into you."

She chewed the last of her breakfast as she looked at the neat script of her sister-in-law's hand on their personalized note cards.

"I wasn't aware that you ever needed an excuse."

"True enough. Paul Bendette deserves better than your behavior."

She stood up, but he took her wrist and turned it over, looking at the scar. There was the old Chandler laugh, long and hearty.

Bay gave him a disgusted look.

"Only you, Whitney Bay, cold pick up a security guard in Newport and wind up with the pediatrician in your hometown."

She yanked back her hand. "It's all your fault, Jem. You and your stupid suggestions. Would you please get your carcass to work now, and leave me alone."

"Not a chance." He picked up her coffee cup and drank from it. "Unlike the other men in your life—and there seem to be hordes—I am in for the duration. You can't divorce me or get rid of me by taking a cruise with your ex-husband."

"Is that what Paul thinks?"

Jeremy put down the mug and stood up. "Isn't it enough that Breck broke you into little pieces? Using Paul to get back at him is childish and it hurts."

She started to laugh. "You think I'm using Paul to get at Breck. Breck thinks Paul is using me to get at him, and I thought Paul was using me to get at Breck. Ain't love grand." She turned and went to the railing and leaned out over the view. "Men don't hurt, anyway. Not like women. Paul keeps pushing and pushing, trying to make me into something I'm not. I can't help other women when I can't even help myself."

She was angry now, furious at Jeremy for dredging it all up again. "I went sailing on *my* boat, and Breck and I settled a lot of old garbage, which was a surprise. Paul knew and didn't try to stop me."

Jeremy took her arm. "Is that what you expected? Some grand show of force from him to keep you from going? I thought you despised that kind of behavior."

She did, but it wasn't the time to admit it. "No, I didn't expect anything. I wanted time to think, and so did he. It's probably over, anyway." She stared at him, feeling miserable. "He's much too busy for me. Always has been."

"Bay, you've had every Chandler wrapped around your little finger since the day you were born. You were diapered before you were wet and fed before you were hungry and coddled so that when life fell apart, you were totally unprepared to cope. I understand that.

"But, damn it," he continued with hardly a breath, "there's a man in your life who's capable of making you stand up on those gorgeous legs and not only take charge of your own life but touch other people's, too."

"Did Paul tell you how successful I was with Anita Stavos? Do you know?"

Jeremy shook his head, which surprised her. "I don't know who Anita Stavos is, but I do know that it sure looks from here as though you're running back to where it's safe, again."

"Paul wants too much."

"Paul wants you to grow up," Jeremy replied.

The truth stung like a slap. It was precisely what she needed; nevertheless, she put her hand over her eyes.

"And he doesn't need to have his heart torn out for the effort."

She looked up. "For heaven's sake, you make me sound like some femme fatale."

"You forget, Kiddo, I've seen you in strapless satin, flouncing your stuff."

She laughed, her gloom broken. "*You* forget. It was all tissues."

Jeremy kissed her curls and shook his head. "No kidding. And all these years I thought you were built like Linda Carter."

"Wonder Woman, I'm not."

"Paul Bendette thinks so," Jeremy added.

Bay sighed. "Well, I've screwed up everything, and maybe he's added to it."

Her brother got ready to leave. "Some people hide behind sails, some behind a stethoscope. For a perky brunette who grew up around men, you've got a lot to learn."

"And you think Paul's the one to teach me?"

"I think you learn that kind of thing for yourself, with someone like Paul beside you."

"All right, Big Brother, I'm listening."

He started for the stairs. "I hoped you might."

Bay's days of solitude were over. Even if she had felt like brooding, the presence of her parents and family made it impossible. The secluded beach was now alive with the kids, Sunfish, sailboards and rock music.

The *Respite* was gone from the mooring as suddenly as it had appeared. Typical Scofield, she thought, no hello, no goodbye. Neither were there any from Paul Bendette until Sunday morning. She greeted the day as if she were facing a blind date. The sky was puckered with clouds moving across the basin. The race would be a brisk one. Good, she told herself. Maybe they wouldn't have time to talk, just sail.

But, they talked. That is, Paul talked, and Bay listened politely once they had unfurled the sails, got underway and sat thigh-to-thigh, skimming the water.

By the time the three-minute gun sounded, she had heard the details of his week in a stilted conversation full of clinical detail as if she were a colleague.

They had touched on few personal things, and there was a sense of relief when they had to pay strict attention to the beginning of the race. From the committee boat the shots continued at two minutes, one-and-a-half and then every ten seconds until the Scots nosed over the starting line in quick succession.

Conversation was kept to the tasks at hand. The first race was difficult, and by the downwind leg they were in fourth place. With Bay at the helm and Paul ready to move, they prepared to set the spinnaker but wound up losing valuable time when it fouled. There was considerable complaining and yelling before it filled and they steadied out. It cost them precious time, and they finished with the three boats still ahead.

The second race was a slight improvement. The wind steadied off as they began, and the spinnaker behaved. With Paul at the helm and Bay at the sheets, they managed a second place.

Once the races were over and the sails stowed, Bay realized the tension between them was back with no place to go. They were still on the Scot when Paul said, "This isn't working."

Bay turned sharply to see what he was referring to and with a start realized he meant them. "Us?"

"I can't talk to you."

She tried a little humor. "You yelled at me pretty well all afternoon."

It didn't help much. His hand came over her arm. "You know what I mean. You know damn well what I mean. You're not the same since you got off your Morgan."

"How would you know? We've barely seen each other!"

"That's part of it," he said, making no move to call the launch.

"Well, the rest of it, Paul, is that I feel like you're analyzing everything I say, everything I do. No one's done that before, I admit." With the exception of my meddling brother, she added silently.

Before he had a chance to fall into their recent pattern, she continued. "I'm a disappointment, face it. I let you down because I'm not living up to the image you created. You're the one with the fantasy! The trophy you intended to flash in front of Breck isn't what you made her out to be. And you know what? I don't intend to apologize."

He grabbed her arm, making the small boat rock on its mooring. "Is that how you see yourself? A trophy?"

She shook him off. "Yes. Breck took Sheila from you and beat you at quite a few other things. This is your big chance to get even by flashing Bay Chandler under his nose."

He was shaking his head. "Is that what you think?"

"What I think," she replied, "is that I have spent the better part of this affair waiting for you, and what I do on my own time is really nothing to trouble yourself about."

From port to starboard the boat rocked then settled. "As long as I'm in medicine, Bay, someone will need me more than you do. Someone with problems far more serious than yours and mine. Isn't that obvious?"

"I'd say that our problems are pretty serious at the moment. *Real* problems. I wasn't running to Breck; I was using my skills just as you do."

She stopped, looking into the blue eyes reading her. "Do you want me to apologize for the fact that I need support occasionally, that I got into something I couldn't handle well? I needed you, Paul, not because I'm weak but because your expertise would have helped. You weren't available.

"I sailed this week because *my* expertise was needed. You're *never* available and if you want someone who can stand on her own two feet in a situation as traumatic as last Sunday's, then go fall in love with a doctor or a social worker. I've had enough of independence, of 'my own space' and all the other garbage. You want it both ways, and you can't have it.

"My family's back, and I see now how much I want to be part of a whole. I'm tired of belonging to no one but myself. It's boring."

"How does Scofield fit in?"

She was surprised by the question and became thoughtful before she answered. "Ex-husbands don't always blow away with the wind. In this case, we're still tied by business."

"He wants you back," Paul said.

"He wants me back in the islands, if that's what I want. Breck feels guilty about a lot of things, and he wanted to make sure that I didn't leave because of the unpleasantness. This future, this independence that you think is so important for me, might hinge on my staying tied to him by investing in the second boat."

She didn't need to look at him to know how he felt, and she wanted to bring up jealousy and trust, but the launch, full of the other contenders, was pulling up next to them.

In silence Paul helped her out of the Scot, and they rode that way back to the yacht club. They didn't speak again until he stood with her next to the Chandler car.

"Are we looking for things in each other that don't exist?" he asked.

"Maybe things that neither of us can provide." Her heart was pounding, and the harder it hammered, the surer she was that it would break.

"Bay, we come from two different worlds. Maybe I was naive enough to think that it could be bridged."

"It's not economics."

He shook his head. "No, it's philosophy. It's not fair of me to keep trying to mold you into someone else. I see that. You're a free spirit; it's part of what I love so much."

Her eyes were hot and filling with tears, making her blink. And it's a part that's tearing us from each other at the same time! she cried silently. "I was a fantasy," she whispered, "and so were you."

"Maybe we should slow this down a little," he said finally as she opened her car door.

"I think we're already at a crawl." She got in. "Paul!" She swallowed. "How much of this affair has to do with getting back at Breck?"

It was his turn to stand in thoughtful silence. She waited, wanting, knowing he would say "None."

"In the beginning, more than I'm proud to admit to."

She felt as though she'd been stabbed.

"And now?"

"Blueblood, I'm a poor kid from Newport, no matter how shiny the polish. You're the brass ring, darling. I wanted to grab it and show him, show the world what I could do. And in the beginning when I thought you were slumming, I wanted to make you fall in love with me as some juvenile proof that I had that much power over feelings that were entirely new to me."

She looked up at him with her vision blurred. He had not answered her question. She turned the key in the ignition, and he pulled his hands from the car window. "I gave a lot of thought to how to start this relationship off, Bay, and the hell of it is that once I was in it I stopped thinking about how to end it. I don't want to and I never did."

She was gritting her teeth. "Life's full of unpleasantness, isn't it? Why don't you let me have the pleasure of bringing this to a grinding halt? It might make me feel a little better to be in control of my own destiny for once. After all, that's what you've wanted all along, for me to face up to the tragedies in my life. Well, Paul, here's lookin' 'em right in the eye."

She threw the car into reverse, leaving Paul and his foul-weather gear in the dust. Half of the people in the parking lot watched her spin and grind the gears till she was out on the main road and heading for the boathouse.

Monday morning, wearing her one outfit that most approximated business attire, Bay marched across the manicured Chandler property, skirted the privet hedge and caught Jeremy on his way to work.

He grinned at her. "This is an unexpected pleasure. You've even got real clothes on."

She looked disgusted. "Squeeze me in. I'm going to the office with the three of you."

Jeremy's eyebrows arched. "Dare I ask why?"

"No."

Her older brother accepted the silence and eased them up the lane to pick up Christopher and John.

Five days later she was still commuting with them, still going home to a silent phone and still incommunicado with Paul. To her surprise, nine-to-five had far more appeal than it had in earlier years.

She spent the first two days on the loft floor of the Chandler Building with Chris, filing, helping the draftsmen, filling in for the receptionist during the lunch hour. Naval architecture held a built-in fascination for her, and it was not the first time she wished she'd been a better student.

Wednesday and Thursday she let her father give her a taste of the warehouse confusion, although at the height of the sailing season the pressure was off. Wait till winter and spring, he promised her, when the whole world wanted sails in four weeks.

It was there that she came across the complaints, personal requests and vagaries of sailors who kept her family in business. On Friday Jeremy handed her a business letter, typed on bond paper, embossed with a family crest. The owner of a Morgan in Annapolis, Maryland, had torn the batten pockets on his mainsail. Bay read the letter then looked at Jeremy. "He says it's a continuous problem. I say he's got the wrong size battens, or he's stowing incorrectly. Doesn't sound like the sail."

Jeremy nodded. "You're right, but he doesn't want to hear it."

"And?"

Hazel eyes met hazel eyes. "We've made him another mainsail, which I want hand delivered, for PR if no other reason. But the problem will keep recurring if he doesn't see the right solution. Take it down, Bay, sail the boat, check the battens."

Her eyes widened. "Me?"

Jeremy laughed. "You—who knows better? Tell him you're about to invest in your *second* Morgan, spend a couple hours on the Chesapeake. This customer is a big honcho, kid. If anyone can have him eating out of her hand, it's you."

"Right, just like the rest of the men in my life."

Her brother took the letter and folded his arms across his chest. "You brought it up. How are the other men?"

"There aren't any."

"You don't expect me to believe that just because you've had a falling out with the good doctor."

"Jeremy, stop your nosiness and make a reservation for Baltimore. Getting out of town is very appealing at the moment."

With her trip planned for Monday morning, Bay found that her depression lifted slightly. It gave her a chance to focus her attention on something besides the fact that she missed Paul terribly. She wasn't the least bit nervous about facing a fifty-foot yacht in a strange harbor, a yacht owned by a power broker known throughout the financial world.

On Saturday, the day of the clambake hosted by Nancy and Jeremy, the weather was hot and sticky and perfect for lolling on the beach. At four o'clock, in shorts and a halter top, Bay walked across sand in the direction of the party. A sandy stone-lined pit was steaming with the catered feast: layers of potatoes, clams, corn-in-the-husk and lobsters cooked in the seaweed. Nearby were buckets of canned drinks and crocks of butter, waiting to be melted.

There were children at a volleyball net and adults in low chairs, teenagers splashing self-consciously, and her family was there, mingling with everybody. With a glass of wine in her hand she walked to the water, avoiding the play, looking out at the horizon. The *Respite* was back at anchor. She was mildly surprised but nothing more.

"You're not about to throw another pair of shoes into the sea, I hope!"

The sound of Paul's voice, so close, made her spin. She looked at the handsome face she hadn't seen in a week. He was smiling.

"Aren't you chancing another punch in the ribs?" She moved a step away.

He shrugged. "We can't very well ignore each other all night, not when Jeremy and Nancy worked so hard to get us together."

"I think we beat them to it, the first time. We were in an awful hurry, weren't we, Paul?"

He kept his smile, rueful as it was. "Too much of one, Blueblood. I've been doing a lot of thinking this week."

Thirteen

—

First to thine own self be true.''

Bay blinked, waited, and when nothing more was forthcoming, skimmed her toe in the lapping water. What the hell did Shakespeare know? *A lot,* she thought sourly, finally looking back at him. ''Do you mean me or you?''

''I mean us.''

His arm went around her shoulder as they looked at the water. It felt comfortable and welcome. ''Somewhere between *Sea Fever* and the Hippocratic oath, two people are trying to make sense out of what has happened to them.''

Paul continued to talk in a voice that touched her heart.

''Your work has always seemed like play to me, frosting on a frivolous life, the kind of thing you do when you don't want to face reality or have enough money so you don't have to.''

She stiffened and felt his arm tighten, too. ''Wait,'' he added. ''Weeks ago you asked me if I had gone into medicine so I could go back to the old neighborhood and have everyone call me 'Doctor.' I denied it, but damn it, Bay, you have a way of cutting through all the garbage, as you call it. You have a way of looking at me and seeing what no one else ever has.''

She smiled at him. ''And part of you,'' she finished for him, ''just a tiny part, had said years ago 'Okay, Bendette, you'll never have the bucks to play for the rest of your life, so go out and save the world instead.' ''

She sighed, feeling herself soften again, not moving from the warmth of him. ''And you do. You make a difference in the lives of everyone you minister to. So much so, that all the resentment I feel at being left behind, or at least put aside, has to be swallowed. How can I criticize when you're healing children?''

He returned her smile. ''And the more I fell in love with you, the more I hid behind my work, my noble, magnanimous profession, because I can't compete with your life-style. Oh, but Bay, you made me see that it's a real skill for you, a talent, and I have no right to make you give it up. If you belong in St. Thomas, I won't stop you.''

She hugged him then, wrapped both arms around his ribs and pressed herself against him, imagining the various Chandlers whom she couldn't see, murmuring and elbowing each other in approval.

''Paul, you darling man, you've made me face the one dark spot in my life, made me see that what was a tragedy then can be overcome by facing it, not hiding.'' She pulled away enough to look into his face. ''Do you think there's a chance that we're actually good for each other?''

He kissed her, and she imagined the applause. "I'd like to stick around and find out," he said.

They broke apart at the sound of cheers and turned back to the assembled throng, both of them flushed. The cheering, however, was for the unveiling of the food as the seaweed and cover were raked away.

Long after dark and well after Paul had begun to walk Bay back to the boathouse, they said good-night. It was also goodbye for the time being. "I want you back in your own bed tonight," she said with as much reluctance as she saw in his face. "Straightening all this out takes a certain amount of solitude."

He grumbled in agreement. "I would have said fortitude."

"That, too," she replied. "By the way, it did not escape my notice that your beeper was silent tonight."

"I can arrange for that more than I do—more than I have."

She feigned surprise. "Is this a confession?"

"All work and no play—"

Bay put her hand over his mouth. "I don't need a quotation; I need one more passionate kiss to get me through the night."

She got it.

The following morning they had agreed to meet at the boathouse for a late breakfast before the final races of the Midsummer Series. The phone rang at nine.

"Hate me; I deserve it," Paul said.

"You can't make it."

"Bay, this can't be helped. Saturday nights and teenage boys—"

She sighed and held her temper. "It's not the end of the world. I understand."

His voice was cheerful. "The fact that I can't make it is the bad news, darling. There's good news, too."

"They've canceled the race even though the weather is perfect."

He laughed. "I've gotten you a substitute, the best, as a matter of fact."

"The best? Jeremy and Chris are at a wedding—"

"Better than that. I called Breck. He'll meet you at the yacht club. I draw the line at letting you give him my breakfast."

She was silent while she digested the news.

"Bay? I intend for you to win."

"Paul, you didn't have to do this...."

"Yes, I think maybe I did. He's the only one in this town capable of pulling you back into first. I've let you down before; I won't do it again."

Her voice caught in her throat. "I love you, Paul."

His reply was a murmur. "I know. I'll see you by dinnertime."

She was locking the sliding door when the phone rang a second time. It was Anita Stavos. Bay's palms began to perspire.

"Miss Chandler—Dr. Crandall left me with your number—I hope you don't mind."

"Of course not." She sat down on the edge of the bed, her free hand nervously spinning a curl through her fingers. "Are you at home now?"

"Yes," the woman replied, still faltering. "Yes, I am. I need to see you. I thought maybe you might come over."

Bay tried to ignore the plea in her voice and the urgency. She looked at her watch. "I don't know." Be honest, she told herself. "I feel awful about last Sunday. I seem to have made things worse."

She could hear the woman's slow, deep intake of air. "No," Anita said. "No, it was me. I didn't think anyone else—I was—" She cleared her throat, and Bay waited, fighting the dread in the pit of her stomach. "I'm much better, thanks to you."

"If you're better, Anita, it's your own doing, your own strength." There wasn't enough time to prolong the conversation. "Would you like to get together tomorrow?" On Monday I'll be in Baltimore, she realized suddenly. "No—" she interrupted herself "—I forgot I'm going out of town on business. Anita, I have to race this afternoon, but I have another name for you. Would you call Audrey Parker?"

There was more hesitation. "I don't think—not someone I don't know."

Bay made a frantic mental analysis of what she could sacrifice. "Anita, I can be there as soon as the race is over this afternoon. It will probably be dinnertime—"

"I don't know," Anita was saying. "My husband will be home. I was hoping we could talk by ourselves first. It doesn't matter. I'm fine, really." There was so much apology in her voice that Bay found herself apologizing before they had finished the conversation. She hung up reluctantly, but not until she was sure the other woman was all right.

Bay promised herself that, husband or not, she would call Anita from the boathouse the minute she returned. It seemed to be the only compromise they could reach, but it was one that put Bay's mind at rest. She was at the yacht club ten minutes later.

Breck and Marcia were on the dock. Breck rubbed his hands together as she approached. "What an opportunity!"

Marcia punched him lightly. "You do rise to a challenge."

Bay smiled at her. "You don't mind?"

She shrugged. "I gave him permission to call you for the charter cruise. I guess if you didn't get in any trouble in the Morgan, then it would be impossible in one of these tiny things."

Breck looked horrified. "You'll ruin my image, telling my ex-wife I need approval."

Marcia looked from him to Bay. "He's on a long leash."

And Bay looked at Breck. "She is the best thing that's happened to you."

He hurried Bay into the launch. "Remind me to keep you two an ocean apart."

"I appreciate this," Bay said once they'd entered the Scot and set to rigging it.

"You helped me out this week. It's the kind of favor I don't mind repaying. Bendette and I had a nice talk, as a matter of fact." He concentrated on his tasks and then looked at her. "Marry him," he said suddenly.

"Breck—"

"He'll never let you down, like I did. I was wrong about him. The son-of-a-gun really loves you."

It's enough to deal with this, she thought, determined to bring the conversation back to the race.

Once the sails were set, the spinnaker in its bag ready for the downwind leg and the course pointed out to Breck, they set off, joining the fleet.

That her concentration was not what it should have been was not apparent until the warning gun. She tried to calculate as they ducked simultaneously and brought the boat about. "Two minutes," she said.

Breck looked at her. "One, Whit. You're off by a minute."

There was another shot thirty seconds later, proving him right. It was not the kind of error she made. Ever.

Nevertheless, they crossed the starting line with the others, their skills showing as the Scot heeled at its most efficient. Halfway up the first leg, they nosed into first place. They sat, as she had with Paul, leaning out over the water, slicing it with the boat.

She wondered if Anita would call Audrey Parker. She hadn't given her the number. The Parkers' number was listed under Ned's, the husband's, name. Anita wouldn't find it in the phone book.

"Let her out." It was Breck at the tiller, looking at the sail. Bay did as she was told without comment.

She wondered what Anita's husband did for a living, how much support he was giving her and if he were like Ned or more like Breck.

"You're luffing. Jesus, Whit, where's your head?"

She blinked, yanking on the sheet. They slipped back. "Sorry!" she yelled over the wind and the water, concentrating enough to pull them up again by the time they rounded the first mark.

Anita had wanted to talk before her husband got home. There wasn't much emotional support there, probably. Hadn't she as much as said that last Sunday in the hospital? A week ago this very minute.

"Hard a lee!" Breck yelled, preparing to change tacks.

Bay got off the coaming and reached for the tiller. "Give me the boat."

"What?" He looked as though he hadn't heard her correctly.

Bay still had the line to the sail in her hand and as Breck sat on the edge of the boat, she took the tiller, as well. He was shaking his head.

She finished bringing the boat around and then, with Breck swearing and his eyes widening, she continued the arc, letting out the sail and pointing the boat in the direction of the marina. She could feel the eyes of the contenders and could imagine the binoculars trained on them from the committee boat.

Breck had his hand on her arm, but made no move to correct the course. "I know I'm only the crew, but may I ask what the hell you're doing?"

She was grinning as she yelled, "I'm growing up, Breck, and it's about time!"

Once in the anchorage, she sailed right past the mooring, which Breck dutifully pointed out. "Did you miss it or is this part of your dingbat plan?"

They approached the pier, where a very confused Marcia was trotting down the ramp. "Throw her the line," Bay said. "I want to bring the Scot up to the dock."

He did as he was told. With the sails flapping and the bow cleated, they both got off the Scot. Bay hugged Breck and then hugged Marcia. "Come for a drink before you leave town," she said and then looked at her ex-husband. "If you ever loved me, you'll do me one last favor."

He shook his head slowly. "I'm afraid to ask."

She laughed. "Take the Scot for me and furl the sails. You and Marcia can stow the gear, okay?"

They shrugged. "Sure."

"I have a patient to see. It's sort of an emergency."

Breck was watching her carefully. "His or yours?"

"Ours" was the last thing she said before waving them off and running up the ramp to her car.

Whitney Bay Chandler felt good. She felt great, elated, in fact.

Anita Stavos lived in an apartment complex on the west side of Alden's Cove. It was sweltering, cooled by slowly rotating fans in each of the living room windows. It was the kind of day that found most of the other occupants at the beach. Anita apologized when Bay said she should be there, too.

"I haven't been out much since I got home."

Bay nodded. In the course of the afternoon they talked. Talked until Anita cried, and Bay was hoarse. They brought up Audrey Parker and the hospital, Dr. Crandall and Dr. Bendette and every aspect of what Anita considered to be the tragedy of her life.

Bay insisted on staying until Anita's husband returned from what turned out to be a day spent with his family. He was old school, old country, and just short of being openly hostile. It masked an honest fear.

At dusk the weather was more reasonable, and after three beers, so was Nicho Stavos. Anita quietly turned on the lights, and without asking, brought in a cold supper. They ate over animated conversation and Bay could feel a creeping sense of optimism. Nicho held his wife's hand.

Bay didn't look at her watch until the sun was almost down and gasped when she realized it was nearly nine. With a promise to call when she returned from Annapolis, Bay brought the conversation to a close. Anita intended to call Audrey, and Nicho intended to see that Anita got back to smiling.

"I'll let myself out," Bay said, getting up from the couch.

Nicho raised his hand. "I'll walk you to the car. You're alone."

Bay smiled and thanked him.

He opened the door for her and then shook her hand roughly. "Thank you," he said. "Nita's been where I can't reach her . . . thinks I feel nothing when I feel so much.'' He rubbed his eyes then shut the door as Bay got in. ''Don't be a stranger,'' he said.

''I won't,'' she answered and started the engine.

No tears, she thought, driving home and thinking of the evening in terms of the *Stavoses'* crisis. She was fine. She was wonderful! It felt very, very good.

At the entrance to the compound she remembered Paul's promise to be at the boathouse by dinnertime. It was nearly ten. She was driving Jeremy's Triumph again. She really needed her own car, now that she had her own life. She bounced over the gravel, thinking about people who kept regular hours and went on dates when both parties showed up. People who didn't fall asleep on each other and weren't constantly apologizing.

It seemed a little dull.

She honked at the Big House and noted that her own place was lighted. There was a little compact car in the usual spot. The doctor was making a house call, after all.

She took the steps two at a time and found Paul Bendette sitting on the couch, reading one of her magazines. The room was full of the night's sea breeze, and she stood for a moment, watching the slow smile spread across the handsomest face she could imagine.

''I'm home,'' she said.

''I can see that.'' He got up.

''I don't suppose you jimmied the lock to get in.''

''*Moi?* I simply told your folks we had a date and you would be running late. They offered a key.''

''I assume you mentioned that your intentions are honorable?''

He was crossing the room. She rubbed her open palms on her dress.

"They have been honorable from the start, almost."

She gulped. His eyes were bluer than they had been the night before; she was sure of it. "I've been with Anita—"

"I've been with Breck," he said.

"Then you know."

He nodded and stopped, keeping a four-foot distance between them. The space crackled with suppressed desire. "And you're all right?" he asked.

She nodded, too, and smiled. "I'm wonderful."

"And Anita?"

"She'll be all right, too."

The breeze was strong for such a late hour. The weather was changing. From behind her the breeze blew into the room, and she stood before it as she had at Sea Mist, letting it nudge her.

She looked at him, in his jeans and polo shirt, at his bare feet and thick yellow hair, and she thought that he looked just the way she had tried to imagine him that first night.

"I love you, Bay," he said in a quiet voice as he was approaching her. His fingers brushed the strap of her sundress. She was melting.

"For what I did tonight?" She was breathless.

"For what you are to me."

She looked at the scar on the palm of her hand and into the eyes that were raising her temperature by degrees. "I've never been anybody's brass ring before."

He looked as though he might laugh, but she kissed him before he could. Kicking off her shoes, she put her arms around his neck, and he worked the zipper along her spine. "I love you, Paul. I've been afraid to tell you, afraid to need you or anyone else. But I made a difference tonight, again, like I did with Audrey. It's because of you, because you've made me believe that I

could. In too many ways I really have been Cinderella.''

"I've never been anybody's Prince Charming before.''

He did laugh then and swooped her up in his arms,
promising as he made his way toward the brass bed that
they would live happily ever after.

Silhouette Desire

OCTOBER TITLES

GREEN FIRE
Stephanie James

DESIGNING HEART
Laurel Evans

BEFORE THE WIND
Leslie Davis Guccione

WILLING SPIRIT
Erin Ross

THE BLOND CHAMELEON
Barbara Turner

CAJUN SUMMER
Maura Seger

Silhouette Desire

COMING NEXT MONTH

CHOICES
Annette Broadrick

Despite his blindness, Damon could sense the beauty of the woman nursing him after his auto accident. But Elise had been hurt once by divorce. Could he cure her fear of love?

NIGHT TALK
Eve Gladstone

Not just the airwaves crackled when WRBZ hired "Big Gun" Casey Phillips to clean up its programming. Although Julie's talk show was on his hit list, the electricity between them couldn't be denied!

KNOCK ANYTIME
Angel Milan

When a portion of Trina Taylor's novel wound up in Jonathan Castle's computer files, the exchange of data seemed disastrous. So why, when the mess was finally sorted out, did they feel strangely reluctant to part company?

Silhouette Desire

COMING NEXT MONTH

PLAYING THE GAME
Kathleen Korbel

Kelly enjoyed posing as hearthrob Matt Hennessy's "latest", and his passionate attentions only helped. But when his real flame arrived in town, Kelly knew she was playing with fire . . .

YESTERDAY AND TOMORROW
Candice Adams

Different backgrounds had separated them before, but when Jay returned a successful businessman, that old excuse didn't hold water. Could Cynthia forget her mother's prejudice and follow her heart?

CATCHING A COMET
Ann Hurley

Charlie Wilde was guiding a Baja Wilderness Trip in search of adventure, but he soon ran headlong into Andromeda, a blue-eyed natural phenomenon determined to be in on the excitement!

She had everything a woman could want... except love.

Locked into a loveless marriage, Danica Lindsay tried in vain to rekindle the spark of a lost romance. She turned for solace to Michael Buchanan, a gentle yet strong man, who showed her friendship.

But even as their souls became one, she knew she was honour-bound to obey the sanctity of her marriage, to stand by her husband's side while he stood trial for espionage even though her heart lay elsewhere.

WITHIN REACH
another powerful novel by
Barbara Delinsky,
author of Finger Prints.

Available from October 1986.
Price: £2.95. **W❂RLDWIDE**